FRANKIE FINDS A DOT

COOPERATIVE REALM

NICKY PENTTILA

I

FRANKIE FINDS A DOT

CHAPTER
ONE

FRANKIE STYLES OPENED her dream-heavy eyes to see an oversized, shaggy cat-eared monster on her bed. Looming right over her face. Blocking out the soft amber glow of the little round-ball lamp she used as a nightlight. The monster's amber eyes swirled hypnotically in near-dark.

So it was going to be one of those days.

"What?" she croaked.

The short word covered so many possibilities: Why didn't you ping me on the wristcom, Spike? Why is it you waking me up and not the ship's AI—or a shrieking emergency alert? How did you manage to teleport silently into my bedroom again?

That last one was easy. Spike—a creature built for infiltration —could burrow calmly into top-secret underwater lairs or boldly stroll right into the captain's quarters aboard their snowman-shaped interstellar cargo hauler. The cyvlossic—outer part over-sized feline, inner part half-cyborg—made security a theoretical concept more than an actuality.

Also, Frankie didn't lock her doors.

Behind Frankie's sleepy confusion floated the comforting,

faint hum of the Spear's air recyclers, soft as a whisper, mixing with the distant metallic creaks of deck plates flexing gently under maintenance bots. She hoped.

Her cabin's mostly bare interior smelled faintly of tea tree cleanser from yesterday's bot visit, blended with the ghostly echo of Old Peters' herbal cologne: peppery, nostalgic, oddly comforting.

Spike just bumped Frankie on the shoulder. More a shove than a bump, the force of it pushed Frankie almost to sitting. When she sat straight, Spike shifted shuffled behind her and her pillow, crowding Frankie to ensure there would be no retreat back into cozy oblivion.

Bed hog.

"Don't be putting your big old mitten paws on my pillow." Frankie rubbed the sleep-grit out of the corners of her eyes. Her fluffy yellow-as-the-midday-sun duvet slid down past her hips, exposing her shoulders and belly to chill air with only a nearly worn-through "Stellar Bells" T-shirt to protect her.

Cold. So they were still in the night part of the cycle.

"What time is it?" She squinted at Spike.

"Trouble," Spike rasped in her gravel-rough voice, a sandpapered rumble that no matter what she said always managed to sound sinister.

Great.

Frankie swung her feet onto the rubber-pebbled flooring, her bare toes curling slightly as icy ship-floor reality chased off any remaining warmth. Grabbing her wristcom off its magnetic charging cradle on the wall just beside the bed, Frankie snapped it onto her wrist and shook it awake. The wristcom lit up obligingly, and unfolding a blue-tinted floating data screen showing ship status.

Three in the morning, Frankie time.

Hull and cargo—check. Well, no cargo, so that wasn't a problem. Air and engines—fine. Still smoothly on course to reach Smithson Station by late afternoon station-time, just as planned.

Nothing out of the ordinary.

Spike put a front paw on Frankie's shoulder—kinda heavy— and reached her other paw toward the screen. The beans on the bottom of the paw extended like nubs of mini-fingers. Frankie pretended not to notice, so weird.

Spike swiped the display's view to outside the ship. The ship was coasting, steadily decelerating along the usual inter-system transit lane through a field of sparse, glimmering ice asteroids. An empty stretch of peaceful space lay around them like black velvet studded with diamonds.

Except for that blinking, angry-red pinpoint at the very edge of detection, sliding swiftly closer on the long-range scanner display.

Coming in fast.

"Ship," Frankie called, lifting her eyes toward the ceiling panels, strips of softly luminescent blue set against the darker metal above, as if Ship herself weren't always around her. "Can you identify that incoming vessel yet?"

Spike shifted, now fully behind Frankie as she sat stiffly, deepening the indentations in the mattress. Effectively trapping Frankie between thick bands of warmth and worry.

Spike set her second front paw on Frankie's other shoulder. The weight pressed her butt deeper into the kinda thin mattress. When they sat this way, their heads were the same height, not counting Spike's wild froth of fur. She needed a new bed.

"Skolls," Spike growled.

"Not even funny," Frankie said, pulse skittering into a higher gear. No way it was the Skolls. They'd been avoiding her—and she'd been avoiding them—since that time a Skoll ship fired on the Spear. Hadn't worked out for the Skolls, who lost that ship when the Galactic Patrol confiscated it for fomenting mayhem too close to a transit jump-tunnel.

Frankie flung the so-soft, so cozy, duvet away from her and stood, dumping her furry colleague untidily off her shoulder. If trouble was knocking this fine morning—or whatever this was—she wanted to answer fully clothed.

And fully caffeinated.

Yesterday's black cargo pants lay rumpled at her feet, only one day dirty. Frankie sadly skipped past her soft slippers with fluffy insides, and padded the three steps to her wardrobe. Next to the tall, narrow duraplast double cupboard where she kept her no-days-dirty clothes sat the sturdy boots, the ones with reliable grav-magnets built into their chunky soles. Good in emergencies, especially when the gravity went wonky.

What this emergency boot territory?

As Frankie wrestled her hands into the long sleeves of a clean, soft cornflower-blue tunic hanging neatly in the cupboard—thanks, bots—the ship's mellow female voice floated into the cabin.

"Captain," Ship said, "the vessel is shaped like a Galactic Patrol cruiser, but has engine signatures and utilizes communications channels common to Skoll Shipping."

Frankie twisted free of the tunic neck snug around her throat, gaze flicking back to Spike.

Her fuzzy colleague was still manipulating the floating screen, paws delicately moving the data, eyes narrowed and intense, fur subtly bristling. Spike looked to be frowning.

If oversized cat monsters could frown.

"They're not going to just pass on by, are they?" Frankie said, grim.

Spike spared her the briefest sidelong glance—a perfect picture of feline disdain—and went back to pushing data around on Frankie's screen.

Frankie slammed her feet into the grav-boots and clicked the magnets to standby. The hug of her heels snuggling into the synthetic padding eased her heart a little.

One of the Spear's little service bots marched in the open bedroom door, one of the spidery ones with electromagnetized legs that didn't reach her knee. It scuttled forward, carrying a steaming mug smelling richly of coffee in two of its legs. Frankie accepted it gratefully, letting the bitter-sweet steam soothe the tightness in her face.

Blessings, little bot.

She sat back on her extra-firm mattress edge to check the seals on her boots. The glowing sun of a duvet still radiated comforting residual warmth beside her.

No time for that, now.

There was no reason for the Skolls to be interested in her right now.

Or ever.

There was no one else out here. No trading outposts nearby. Nobody at all.

They had to be here for her.

Wonderful.

"Ship, please contact SystA and start streaming a running secure-data feed now." If they got blasted into atoms, her boss would at least know why.

"I hate waiting," she said to Spike. "Let's call them first."

Spike flicked her paw, shoving the floating screen through the air toward Frankie. She'd already prepped the comm system, the Skoll ship's ping blinking expectantly.

Frankie opened a direct comm along their preferred band.

"Hey, Skoll ship," Frankie said, pushing false calm into her voice. "Nice to see you!"

Silence stretched just long enough to tighten Frankie's spine. Then a low, flat voice returned: "Spear. Prepare to be boarded."

Better and better.

TWO

FRANKIE DIDN'T LIKE the idea of her ship being boarded. By anybody, really, but certainly not the Skolls.

After she pushed Spike farther up the bed and out of direct visual line, Frankie expanded the communication channel to transmit visual from her cabin. She'd preferred comms from the pilot's room, where the sleek consoles and nice seats lent professional presence—but there wasn't time. And the Skolls didn't deserve it.

"Hi!" Frankie said brightly, forcing calm into her voice and a cheerful expression onto her probably sleep-lined face. "I'm captain of the cargo ship Spear, just making our usual run toward Smithson. What's up?"

The Skolls did not open a visual channel.

Creeps.

The voice was that of a Skoll, or Skoll-wannabe: low register, blunt, not musical at all. "We are seeking a cargo," they said. "We expect it is on your ship."

Not "suspect." Expect.

Interesting.

Frankie forced a casual shrug and a mildly puzzled expression. "Sorry to disappoint, but we're dead-heading to Smithson. I've got nothing at all."

"That is irrational."

"Only cargo going out this way was glimmerantin beans," Frankie said. Thanks to the Skoll's near-monopoly on edge-space shipping. "Last time I hauled glimmerantin, the cleanup was more expensive than the profits. Those beans aren't worth the stink."

"Irrelevant."

Frankie blinked twice at their dismissiveness. "Hey, you brought it up. Anyway," she repeated, firm. "We're empty, so there's nothing to find."

A thick pause. Frankie stared at the flat black visual relay on their side, imagining that flat voice belonging to a giant green snake, wrapped around one of those tall snake-stands that look like trees. Tasting the air.

The toneless voice returned. "Prepare to be boarded. We must inspect."

In the corner of Frankie's floating screen, the scanner overlay tracked the incoming vessel as it catapulted toward her. Enormous, at least eighteen times the mass of her squat snowman ship. And probably eighty times faster, too. Especially with Spear's engines throttled down on gentle coast.

"No," she said.

Now the voice had a tone. Freezing cold. "You allow boarding protocol, we lock briefly onto your hull, and you go on your way. Alternately, we hook you, and drag you into our ship, and your transit to Smithson is deeply delayed."

Put it that way.

"We understand," the Skoll-voice continued, "you have live produce waiting at Smithson. Perishable cargo. Cannot afford delay."

Frankie scowled and crossed her arms tightly across her tunic. Then she remembered the Skolls were getting full visual and wiped the screen to cut off her camera. She looked at Spike, lounging on her pillow, licking a paw.

"Ideas?"

Spike tilted her shaggy head a little, eyes half closed.

Sure would be nice to have a colleague who liked to talk and didn't expect you to just read their minds.

Frankie sighed—then suddenly brightened with inspiration. Caffeine must have kicked in. She flicked open the camera again.

"Neither," she said on the open channel.

"Captain Styles—" the Skoll growled.

Captain. She still loved how it sounded, even coming from these jokers. A proper title for the owner of a ship, even one crewed by nosy bots and a cranky hybrid cyvlossic.

"Hear me out," Frankie said. "We both know you carry heavy-duty scanners that can see clear through my hull as if it were made of glass." Illegal scanners. Military-grade, and no little insult to Galactic Patrol regulations. "So scan us. We have nothing to hide."

Spike abruptly jumped off the bed and ran out the door, turning toward the kitchen and piloting section.

Or maybe one of them did have something to hide.

"Possible," the Skoll acknowledged after another lengthy pause.

Frankly smiled thinly. "That way, you, too, can keep moving. Convenient and fast."

The pause was even longer. Frankie sipped her coffee, inhaling deeply the rich, faintly bittersweet steam. The bots had used the good beans.

On the map corner of the floating screen, the big ship was closing in fast.

While she waited, her restless gaze tracked around her dull-gray wall panels, so depressingly neutral and plain. She needed to decorate her space. Not re-decorate, since she'd never really decorated in the first place. It was purely functional, this space. Just the bed, a gray-box of a nightstand, and the tall wardrobe-dresser unit that was crowded the corner opposite the head of the bed. Gray, of course.

Maybe cream walls—a pale, buttery tone—would warm the space. Match her little glow-globe light. Paint the wardrobe something vivid to match the cheerful sunny yellow of the duvet. A sky blue, or cornflower, like her tunic.

Then she could match her room.

Maybe not.

The Skoll voice returned finally, sharp but amenable. "Acceptable. Five minutes to scan."

Seriously? They had to be that close to her to activate the scan?

Or they just needed to pretend that they did.

FRANKIE SWIPED THE SCREEN CLOSED. Coffee snugly in hand, she moved swiftly down the hallway—dull gray —and toward the more-welcoming kitchen area. As her sturdy booted footfalls rang softly against the rubber-coated metal plating, she pictured brightening this corridor, too. No cream here; busy working hallways needed easy-maintenance colors. Maybe spearmint green, clean and bright—

Maybe Ship had opinions on color schemes?

Then again, Ship hadn't yet been able to come up with a name for herself, so maybe not.

Too many choices.

Spike had already commandeered her side of their favorite table by the time Frankie arrived. Perched regally on the back of the three-sided eating nook, she licked a paw casually as if she hadn't just bolted through the ship on who-knew-what errand.

At least she'd left the sun-bright orange bench cushions free for Frankie.

Small comforts.

"Five minutes to scan," Frankie said, setting her coffee on the nook's smooth-but-always-sticky-looking table. Gray. "Breakfast?"

Spike gave her a look. Frankie glanced around the narrow, neatly arranged galley—long L-shaped counter of dark, practical composite, supplies neatly stacked against the upper walls or tucked under the counter in extruded gray plasmetal cabinets. At the cyvlossic-only side dining area, a knee-high shelf set opposite their nook between the kitchen cabinets and the fridge-freezers. Two empty plates remained, scattered with crumbs.

Breakfast had already been served.

Frankie crossed over to the cold storage and pulled out yester-day's leftover noodles and set them into the reheater. The warm air abruptly intensified with the aromas of peanut and ginger—a tangible reminder of last night's snack experiment gone awry. Sticky sauce had rained onto distant counter corners. The non-caramel corn she'd created was delicious, even if spots still lingered stubbornly behind the counter's reheater unit.

While her noodles sputtered, Frankie retrieved a tofu crunch bar, settling back in resigned comfort onto the bright cushion, her half-full steaming coffee in front of her. The kitchen was cozy warm. Ship must have decided it was daytime now, no matter what the actual time.

She felt nothing physical when the Skoll scan began. Lucky she lacked the cursed sensitivity some spacers complained of, describing scanner waves crawling like static under their skin.

The "we're done" ping from the Skoll ship came soon enough.

"Spear. You are clear."

Frankie swallowed fast, curry noodles warm and fragrant in her throat. "Apology accepted," she replied thickly. "So what are you looking for, anyway? We'll keep an eye out."

"A sentient individual. We detect none aboard your ship."

Ouch.

Spike snorted.

"Fantastic!" Frankie said over-enthusiastically. "See you around, then!"

The Skoll ship—registered as the Blasted Parts, according to Ship—accelerated abruptly. It flashed past them into deeper space.

Frankie exhaled relief. "Well, that's done," she said.

She could not have been more wrong.

CHAPTER
THREE

THE SKOLL SHIP wasn't their only visitor on the last leg of their trip to Smithson Station.

Not four hours after that joyful interaction, Frankie lay flat on her back under the cramped counter in the pilot's room, shoulders pinched painfully between the curve of a metal casing and the solid square of support for the copilot's seat. She squinted upward in disbelief.

How had Spike managed to shed enough fur in here to clog the backup navigation boards? And why, exactly, did those tufts smell faintly—annoyingly—of musty incense?

The ping of an incoming comms hail startled her. Nobody should be anywhere near. She sat up fast, and her forehead collided with the underside of the counter, causing red blooms of pain to flash across her vision.

"Ship," she said, "tell them I'm coming."

She scrambled up into the wide pilot's seat, flicked power switches on the console, and stared blearily at the five-monitor array. A crisp stack of blue-edged screens set neatly against matte gray composite. Designed to be functional and comfortable, the pilot's room, at the end of the hall on the crew level of the ship, had a snug kidney-bean shape. Two chairs, wide enough for a cyvlossic to curl up and nap in. Behind, on either side of the sliding door to the hallway, sat the two emergency escape pods, not the sphere kind but the kind that looked like eclairs.

The space was cozy enough during regular ops but packed a little tight when repairs were involved. While the Spear could be piloted from anywhere—and Ship, really, did most of the piloting—this was where you wanted to be for the fancy stuff.

Frankie brushed stray fur from the controls, momentarily distracted as it swirled lazily in the gently shifting air currents.

And landed in her lap.

Spike padded silently through the open door, her shaggy bulk moving like a ghost. She jumped onto the copilot seat and regarded Frankie with a calm look of bland disinterest. Her matted fur stood stiffly in clumps, its stripes barely visible beneath the tangled mess.

An incoming craft had swung out from the shadow of a nearby asteroid. The Spear's bottom two big monitors tracked it clearly, showing it swiftly matching speed alongside their slower cargo hauler.

Another Galactic Patrol-style vessel. Great.

Frankie remembered a time when the G.P. were the only ones who had these monster ships. Should've known it couldn't last, especially out here in edge space. Couldn't be good that the Skolls were the first to grab one, though.

The Galactic Patrol held power over the jump-gates and in the Central Cooperative Space districts. But star systems were big. Plenty of stuff just slid on by the Cooperative Realm's premier defenders.

She rubbed her forehead—she was going to have a bruise—when the verbal hail came through.

"Spear, this is the Ever Ready." Still, officious. We have a delivery for you."

"Ever Ready," Frankie replied cautiously, watching Spike stretch out, her big paws kneading lazily at the worn orange upholstery of the seat. "You sure about that? We're not expecting anything."

"Right. I have something to say, where is it?" The voice suddenly sounded a lot less authoritative. Like a teenager pretending they were the comms chief or something. "Ah. Um. Itsy-bitsy spider bites?"

Frankie's eyebrows lifted slightly. An imaginative little code phrase that screamed Systems Analysis. Apparently, Bruce was back on his fairytale kick.

Systems Analysis was officially a data-processing company charged with gathering, analyzing, and disseminating critical information across Cooperative Space. Unofficially, it rescued lost people, made sure bad actors had worse luck, and generally tried to make this slice of the galaxy a better place.

To do this, SystA employed an eclectic mix of people (and cyvlossics) whose talents might not be recognized—or welcomed—elsewhere. Spike had recruited Frankie to SystA after their near-fatal run-in with the Skolls.

It was working so far.

She flashed Spike a meaningful glance. "Heard from Bruce lately?"

The cyvlossic tilted her head the slightest bit, eyes noncommittal. Meaning yes. Probably. Maybe.

Would be really nice if opinions around here came via words instead of subtle matted-fur body language. Frankie tried to stop bugging at the new and growing bump on her forehead and focus on the situation at hand.

"Ever Ready," she said. "We stand corrected. Thank you for the package. Going to port it over?

"Capsule send," they replied in their grownup voice."You can keep the capsule. It came with the package."

Frankie frowned at Spike, who had sat up again, her raggedy ears twitching forward at this interesting tidbit.

"What's in the package?"

"Dunno," back to teenager voice, sheepish.

Apparently, Galactic Patrol was far more trusting than she was.

"Great," Frankie said. "Point it at the cargo bay—the big bottom bulb. I'm lighting up the outer bay doors now."

"Capsule away. Ten minutes to arrival."

Frankie closed the comms channel and looked at Spike.

The matted fur around the shoulders. The tufts that screamed for brushing. All camouflage when Spike was out hunting information in places only mid-sized four-legged creatures could reach. But here, it was just gross.

"Hey, how about a spa day?" Frankie said. "We go in the greenhouse room and get all steamed up, and then I brush your hair and you brush mine." Frankie's straight, dark hair was currently slashed at an angle from just below her left ear down to her right jaw.

Spike lifted a paw and licked the tip. Four dagger-like claws popped out from those deceptively velvet-looking pads.

Then she hopped off the chair, padding quickly out and down the hall. Headed for the cargo bay.

Frankie hurried after. "Because fur in the nav boards is totally normal and not bad at all!"

Spike was already past the kitchen. She wasn't running, but she got to the end of the hall and punched the floor panel to open the first door of the airlock to the cargo bay before Frankie had even reached her captain's rooms, halfway there. She had to slide to make it past the door before it cycled closed. They didn't need to vent the air—the cargo hold had some—but just cycled through the second door.

The cargo bay spread before her dark, enormous, echoingly cold. No gravity.

Gripping the handhold next to the outer airlock door, Frankie powered up the sparse lane of running lights along the inside of the hull; they seemed to vanish into the distance. She illuminated the bump of the big airlock that led to the larger set of bay doors.

It looked tiny from here.

Her breath steamed in ghostly patterns before vanishing. They maintained about a half-standard air balance in here and a minimal warmth to keep the plants they usually portered alive. It was like a trip to the tallest mountains to come in here—sharp ozone scent, crisp and cold enough to burn exposed skin.

The tallest mountains without much gravity.

She checked that the retractable metal walkway was locked. The walkway—a finely-strutted metal-mesh gantry fringed with sturdy handrails, stretched straight out into the chamber. It could extend almost the length of this cavern of a hold, so she could get to cargo wherever it was without float-bouncing all over the place. At the moment it was was just a stub of itself, only ten meters or so.

She stepped onto its metal grid floor, clicking her grav boots on, and then let go of the handhold. She reached back to grab one of the long orange puffy coats hooked to the wall beside the controls.

Mittens in the pockets, yeah.

Spike hovered at Frankie's hip. Like a giant dust ball, each strand of fur fully extended. The cyvlossic could move in no-grav like it was water. Didn't make sense, but there it was.

Frankie pushed forward with steady steps, looking for the first set of tie-downs. Not so much a rope and hook, but a pair of retractable docking clamps on either side of a gate in the guard rail that could swing in. They mostly used the tie-downs for delivering personal cargo, like food and printer supplies.

But it was also the right size for a standard escape capsule.

"What do we do with another capsule?" Frankie asked Spike as the docking lights shifted from purple standby to green readiness. "Use it instead of the shuttle?" It wasn't as fast as their box of a six-seater shuttle bus, but probably used way less juice.

Spike hunkered near the floor of the walkway, watching the cargo bay door. Ignoring her.

The outer airlock lights went purple. Its inner doors slid open. A scarred, gray globe capsule floated slowly out. It oriented itself to the lights on the gantry, propulsion units hissing faintly, and headed toward them. Its propulsion needed tuning; she could hear the whining from here.

The steam of Frankie's breath sighed out, as if reaching through the dark cold to greet the capsule.

"Or we could put it at the tip of the engine sphere," Frankie said. The Spear was three stacked spheres: a small engine and mechanics sphere, a middle-sized living and working area, and this mammoth cargo bay. "Like a nose on a snowman."

Spike didn't say anything. Pointedly.

The whoosh-chug of the capsule eased as it slowed for docking. It had the usual double stripes of lights paralleling around its diameter. The usual three dish-shaped antennas strategically placed. But it wasn't labeled. No ship's name, no hauler logo, nothing.

Maybe that's why it looked so beat up. Nobody was taking care of it.

It had oriented itself to have its main door facing the walkway. The tie-down clamps caught it and eased it into position against the walkway. A whoosh in the back as the propulsion shut itself down.

Burnt plastic odor leaked through the air as Frankie doublechecked the clamps. She swung the guard rail in, and touched the capsule's door.

Sub-ice cold, like it should be. Lucky for mittens.

She hesitated just briefly—should've scanned it, really—but her hand had already punched the door release. Too late to panic now. Right?

Stepping warily backward, Frankie felt Spike's reassuringly bulky shape hovering near her hip. The wariness mirrored in those amber eyes fixed unwaveringly on the capsule as its door spiraled slowly, silently, upward.

Slightly warmer air brushed her face from inside the capsule, carried on the slight breeze from the door's opening.

Nothing else happened.

Duh.

A shipment, not a monster.

Frankie edged cautiously forward, tension tight across her shoulders. Just cargo. Stay calm.

Spike stayed where she was, hunched down on the walkway.

Something dark gray and casket-shaped was laid across the circle of bucket seats that ringed most of the inside of the capsule. Frankie clicked on the interior lights.

An escape pod. Inside another escape pod.

Weird kind of shipping container.

Maybe it was parts for some special surgery? Or even a person? Needing transport to Smithson for emergency care?

But Galactic Patrol would have done that.

No they wouldn't. They didn't know what was inside the capsule.

Why would SystA ship them escape pods?

Maybe it was somebody rich who had to get to Smithson but hated space travel.

Or…

Someone who maybe didn't want to scan as "sentient human." The capsule would have read as non-human contents to standard scanners.

Frankie stepped closer.

The pod was on.

With, yes, a whole entire person inside.

CHAPTER
FOUR

FRANKIE LEANED CLOSER, her breath clouding the coffin-sized escape pod's transparent faceplate. Through the now-frost-rimmed window, she could see the peaceful face of a female-presenting person. The delicate bones of her face painted faintly silver-blue by the soft, pulsing glow of internal status lights. Her brown skin glittered faintly with frost crystals sprinkled along her jawline.

Cryo-freezer.

"It's somebody," Frankie called back to Spike, whose quiet breathing puffed audibly in the frigid, near-silent cargo hold.

The sleeper's long, intricate braid lay draped tidily along one shoulder of a standard-issue cream-colored spacer undersuit.

Secured to the bucket seat nearest the capsule's entry, hung a matching outer boots-and-suit and top-of-the-line-helmet. Cream accented in reflective black, nice. Probably sized just for her, too.

The seats next to that were spilling over with three identical hard-sided pieces of rolling luggage, bright green.

Why would Bruce send them a person? A frozen one, even?

Spike shuffle-floated into the escape pod. The cyvlossic

pushed off the pod's floor gently, but not gently enough. No-grav gave an extra oomph to every move. She flew past Frankie's head in a cloud of incense-smelling fluff, pivoted, dampened her bounce on the ceiling of the capsule and slowly floated down to the top of the box. Big huffs of steamy air puffed around her head.

Frankie, grateful for her grav-boots, refrained from comment.

"Know her?" she said.

Spike pressed her furry face close to the pod's little window. Her ears perked forward, her eyes narrowed briefly. But after a moment, she shook her big shaggy head. Carefully, in the no-G.

"Think we're supposed to wake her up?" Frankie placed her free hand on top of the pod. The casing vibrated softly, giving reassurance more than answers. The control panel's calm all green readouts whispered that everything was within normal parameters.

Nothing about this was normal.

"Ship," Frankie spoke into her wristcom, her voice a quick echo in the sphere-pod, a longer one in the gigantic cargo bay itself. "Would you scan this container. Can you find out who this person is in the pod?"

A pause followed—unusual for Ship, who was usually instantly responsive. Finally: "There are two confirmed life-signs in the cargo bay. Human and cyvlossic."

Frankie furrowed her brow and aimed a questioning glance at Spike, who flicked one tufted ear dismissively. "So what does the little pod scan as?"

"Glimmerantin beans."

Ha. Ha.

Spike snorted steam through her moist black nose. "Call Bruce," she rumbled.

FRANKIE SWIFTLY ACTIVATED a secure comm channel via her wristcom, silently blessing Systems Analysis—SystA—for providing the galaxy's fastest real-time comm link. Usually, Bruce never picked up directly; this time his booming voice surprised her, filling the quiet space in an instant.

"Team!" Bruce's voice roared even from the tiny speaker in Frankie's wristcom.

Frankie winced, dialed down the speaker volume, and tried unsuccessfully to tuck her rapidly numbing toes deeper under the hem of her thick cargo-hold coat. Should've moved back into the warm section of the ship first.

"Got your package, Bruce. Want us to reheat?"

"Package secure?"

"Cargo hold, locked down."

"Outstanding. Leave it chilled until you reach the base."

The base? "We're headed toward Smithson," she said. "Station?"

"Then you'll be bouncing." Bruce glanced away, humming—cheerfully off-key—the familiar lullaby about a certain spider and its aquatic adventures for a moment. "There."

Frankie's wristcom pinged; incoming encrypted file. She shook up a thin floating data-screen. Spike tilted her head and looked hard right—must have gotten the message, too. Cyvlossics—at least this cyvlossic—had various tech implants that served various functions that they did not wish to discuss. Frankie was pretty sure Spike could send and receive text and other data files, as well as see in the dark.

Frankie skimmed the message. "Never heard of this place." Base Twelve—a joke, surely—was three jump gates away from Smithson. Nowhere near their usual route. Frankie didn't think she'd ever been in that stretch of space. Certainly not piloting.

"Most people call it White Moon Landing," Bruce said casually.

The chill sneaked through the jacket and locked onto her shoulders.

"Wait—the toxic research site? The contaminated disaster zone?"

Bruce chuckled, unperturbed. "Not so much. A research site that the Cooperative doesn't want anyone sniffing around."

"Co-op? Direct?"

"Through a shell company."

The cold seemed to come from inside Frankie's body.

"Not Orr Industries." Killers. Casual killers, which was worse.

"No." Bruce's voice softened, suddenly earnest. "Orr is nowhere near this one. Luckily, because we need both your sets of skills."

Frankie resisted a bitter laugh. What skills? A brief flare of childhood fame frozen forever around eight-year-old Frankie Styles, poster child for the Orphans of Wala? She was thirty now; nobody gave her a second glance anymore. At least so long as she kept her hair short. And stayed away from Central District.

Whatever her skills were, they'd gotten her this weird on-call not-really-a-side-gig that she couldn't ever talk about. Systems Analysis was a boring corporate shell company on the outside, and a hive of secret do-gooders on the inside. Bruce sent her on missions to rescue damsels, frustrate villains, quietly improve outer-rim welfare. And promise never to say a word about it.

Frankie could talk all she wanted about the cargo hauling she did as a cover, but nobody was ever interested in that. Wearing cargo pants and concert T-shirts and hauling boring freight hither and yon never drew a second glance.

Well, except from Skolls with black-market scanners.

Frankie silently longed to leap into action, despite shivering from head to toe. Guess that made her a do-gooder, too.

"Fine," she said. "Twist my arm."

"Listen up," Bruce said. "Package is time-sensitive. Stop at

Smithson only long enough to be seen on cameras. Pick up some of that good ramen on second level. Then go."

Frankie nodded. "And, um. Do we defrost?"

"Later," Bruce said decisively. "Wait until you've cleared the gates and sighted the station. When your ship confirms visuals, then start the warming cycle. She'll need hours. Handle carefully after. The package, awake, does not enjoy gravity transitions."

Which was a good reason to travel long-distance as an icicle rather than a person. Gravity sickness was a beast.

Frankie skimmed the rest of Bruce's briefing. Took no time: beyond the map and landing coordinates, there wasn't anything else.

"Any prep notes?"

"After the last jump," Bruce replied, secretive as always. "But pick up some sweets—those honey gummies—from Smithson's market stalls. Makes an excellent gift."

Frankie's mittened fingers brushed again over the softly vibrating pod casing.

So much for routine cargo runs.

CHAPTER
FIVE

HONEY GUMMIES TURNED out to be plentiful on Smithson Orbital Station. Of course they did. Horse racing was practically religion on the planet below, and apparently, racing enthusiasts had a severe sweet tooth. Frankie paid a premium for six small, sleek, brightly labeled boxes, the credit carefully deducted from their station account. Yet the entire time she lingered aboard Smithson, not-so-casually strolling the brightly lit market concourse under the security cameras' indifferent watch, Frankie felt like a thief.

Actually, she'd felt criminal ever since the mysterious cryo-coffin pod had parked itself inside her ship.

Leaving a person, frozen or not, alone in her cargo hold had twisted knot after uneasy knot in her gut. People weren't cargo. Cargo didn't have long elegant braids, fancy spacer suits, and peaceful faces smoothed gracefully in sleep. Cargo didn't haunt her dreams.

People had names. Stories. Secrets.

And they were so, so fragile.

Frankie tried to talk herself down by picturing the situation as if the person was like her, when she was having one of her horror-show days. On those days, when the PTSD raged, sometimes it was comforting to take the fuzzy orange blanket and tuck herself into one of the escape capsules on the pilot's deck. Pull the lid down almost all the way. Alone, and safe. Quiet but for the usual ship's pulsing. Warm. Kinda womblike.

Except the person in the cargo bay was so terribly cold.

Except no, they weren't. They didn't feel anything. Totally asleep.

But were they dreaming?

Frankie's history with nightmares offered another disturbing thought. What if her guest was trapped in frozen dreams, helpless to wake themselves out of some nightmare?

Ugh.

Immediately after buying the gummies, Frankie wasted no time lining up her slot for the first jump gate. Only an hour to wait. Back aboard, she told Ship to make all possible speed to the second and third. The sooner the defrosting began, the sooner she could stop fixating on it.

Seventy-three almost sleepless hours later, the Spear popped out of the third gate and into the sector that held White Moon Landing. Frankie was completely exhausted, Spike openly exasperated at her restlessness.

The package in the cargo bay was unchanged.

As the Spear started the deceleration toward White Moon Landing, Frankie had the medium-sized crablike cargo bots scuttle out the freezer-coffin to the medical suite, a place she'd barely stepped foot in since she'd bought the ship. Frankie hadn't needed it in all the months she'd been captain, touch duraplast.

Old Peters, the cargo hauler's first owner, had fitted the space up nice. He needed it, what with all the war injuries and "plain ole gettin' on." Which was also why there were foot panels beside all the doors, top and bottom. And all the cupboard drawers opened with a slight push, no handles needed. Stairs and elevators and even a zip-tube to get from floor to floor. Frankie sometimes thought the only reason Spike put up with her as a partner was that the Spear could accommodate cyvlossics as comfortably as low-mobility people.

The medical suite was top-notch, meticulously adapted for senior bodies and occasionally-limited mobility. Frankie watched gratefully as the clever bots, almost invisible beneath the bulky pod, maneuvered gamely through the suite's gently gliding double doors and wide, accommodating spaces.

Medical here meant comfort. Meant safety.

The medical suite smelled faintly of dust and menthol. Frankie tapped the wall controls, dialing up the temperature until she felt the return airflow warm to nearly sweating, just how Spike preferred it. Too warm for Frankie's taste.

But the person would be freezing.

The room was perfectly square, white duraplast walls faintly reflective like cloudy mirrors. Thick retractable curtains—now neatly rolled into discreet ceiling and floor tracks—could slice the room neatly into private and sterile halves at will. Frankie left the curtains where they were. No need for sterility, or secrecy. Just warmth, space, and readiness.

Two ample medical beds sat side-by-side, their pristine white mattresses topped by cheerful fluffy duvets the same vivid orange as the cushions in the kitchen. Their narrow headboards were of sturdy dark composite, styled for utility but not ugly. Small panels inset at the top corner of each headboard were silent now but when necessary could light up with life signs.

Opposite the beds stood the med-room's serious tech: surgical carrier arms, auto-surgery robotics poised silently, sterile dark gray instrument panels sealed tightly behind transparent covers. All seemed to be sleeping, patiently awaiting the day Frankie would need them. Hopefully never.

At the back of the room stood ranks of flush-mounted gray cabinets, their minimalistic doors smoothly integrated. No handles, just gentle press-points. A central doorway between cabinets led to a discreet back-room hallway. Frankie checked that too: a generous shower and toilet area—clean, white tile, stocked with thick plush towels in shades matching the duvets—faced another narrow storage nook stuffed neatly with folded blankets, fresh bedding, and stacked chairs in case of visitors.

Feeling oddly maternal, Frankie had laid her own plush orange robe and cozy slippers on top of the second bed, along with bulbs of fresh water and clear bags brimming with salty-savory biscuits, sweet dried fruits, and grainy umami protein chips within easy reach. Who knew what unfrozen guests would want first?

The bots set their cargo on the floor of the medical room to the side of the nearest bed and scurried off.

Frankie knelt beside the pod, placing one hand lightly on its freezing outer shell. She peered inside the faceplate again. Sleeping Beauty indeed. Frost-crystal lashed rimmed delicate closed eyelids. Locks of frozen hair glittered like starlight woven into silk. Frankie smiled softly, enjoying this strange intimacy, the privilege of watching someone sleep.

She slid the protective cover off the pod's small control screen, just beneath the frost-daubed window. A gentle waking, only a few button presses away. So simple looking, for such a complicated bit of tech. Everything on the screen was still green; still "within parameters."

"Revive?" the peaceful blue letters asked.

Frankie took a breath, slowly, heart calming itself. This person deserved safety, peace, warmth. A gentle awakening.

The med-room's door was closed, and the air and particle filters on their own circuit. As clean as she could make it for their visitor.

Frankie pressed the spot on the pad for yes.

A breath's silence. Then the cryo-pod slammed noisily to life. No gentle hum now, the roar coming from some kind of blower at the foot of the pod sudden and violent.

From her kneeling position, Frankie jerked upright instinctively.

Coin-sized holes popped open all down the length of the pod, aggressively venting thick, hot clouds of pungent steam—steam that reeked of rancid socks.

Frankie choked, lungs seizing.

"Ship!" she gasped. "Ventilate!"

Sensors blared muffled warnings that she barely registered amid coughing spasms. Her vision swam, suddenly clouded.

Frankie lurched away, turning for the door. Now her whole mind was clouded, rancid.

She took a step, and then another half step. No door. She must be turned around. Must be facing toward the door to the shower in back, not to the ship's hall.

She was out before her hip hit the floor.

CHAPTER
SIX

FRANKIE WOKE to a bitter-moss mouth and a splitting headache. Her skull pulsed raw aches in rhythm with the slow blink of the dimmed ceiling lights.

That couldn't be right.

Hard floor against her back. Medical suite, right? The cream-colored ceiling was too far away, its soft inset lights not healing afternoon sunshine but caution yellow.

Her lungs burned with every breath. Each shallow inhale ragged as if lined with steel wool. Each exhale just as nasty.

She lay sprawled on the floor. Carefully, Frankie flexed fingers that prickled with sharp, tiny pins. Arms and legs buzzed, clumsy and full of wool, like somebody else's arms sewn awkwardly onto her body.

Great job, Frankie. Get gassed on your own ship.

At least medical care was just an arm's reach away.

At least, if she could get up.

She forced herself onto hands and knees, a tentative move that triggered instant rebellion among the delicate bones in her inner ears. Nausea surged, hot and ugly. Frankie froze, stilled her breathing, waited patiently until the dizziness grudgingly passed. Soon enough, immediate vomiting was downgraded to uneasy quease.

Better. Ish.

A wall might be nice, to lean on.

Inch by inch, Frankie shuffle-crawled toward the blur that suggested solid support, her brain-fluff craving stability. The streamlined medical cabinets along the far wall were closest—gray, austere, and clinical, not so friendly now. She carefully levered her spine against the cool smooth surface, the contact pressing the door to open against her back. She pressed the door again to close it, bumping her head lightly against the cabinet's edge. Pain spiked briefly, then faded, lost among all her other aches.

Great job, sitting up.

She drew a cautious, deeper inhale, testing the air for the earlier stomach-turning stink of burnt socks and chemicals gone bad. Clean, filtered ship-air filled her abused lungs. Good. At least Ship's filters had worked.

Frankie blinked groggily, her eyes slowly regaining focus.

The pretty lady from the escape pod sat cross-legged and serene on the far bed, watching Frankie coolly. Her long ink-black braid, perfectly ordered, cascaded gently across her shoulder, nearly touching her hip. Her clean spacer undersuit was crisp cream against the vivid orange duvet beneath her.

The killer cryo-pod on the floor behind her had closed.

Frankie frowned thickly. Cryo-pod people always woke soggy, confused, ragged. This woman looked shockingly clean and neat.

She must have showered, in that back room.

She would have had to step right over Frankie to do it.

Bitch.

"Welcome back," the woman said, polite, as if she were offering tea. Pleasant alto, if a bit reedy.

Frankie thought about raising her hands, in surrender or askance, but just the thought made her tired. Besides, whoever this was, she clearly could see that Frankie posed no threat.

"Poison?" Frankie rasped, her voice harsher than Spike's morning growl.

"Defensive aerosol, actually." The woman's eyes were soft brown but her expression was steely. "Standard anti-piracy measure. You'll be fine. The scrubbers in here are excellent. Here." She leaned forward, grabbed a water bulb from the stash on the bed Frankie had left as a welcoming gift, and deftly underhanded it toward Frankie.

Unprepared, Frankie's wool-stuffed arm reacted too late. The soft blue bulb bounced uselessly off her unresponsive biceps, dropping into her lap with an undignified squish.

But water sounded so, so good.

As she tried to get her fingers to all kind of work together to grab it, the woman kept talking. Calm, casual, conversationally deadly.

"The pod's security system was a tad enthusiastic. But necessary, given the current climate. Your ship-friends couldn't help. Contamination protocols, you know. Standard quarantine response." She looked up, and to the left. Checking some neural implant. "Ninety-five percent clean," she said.

Frankie struggled to clear the gravel from her throat. "How long?"

A small, unconcerned shrug lifted the woman's perfect shoulders. "Four hours, give or take. My turn now. Why did you wake me up?"

Frankie had managed to fumble the bulb up to her lips. She squeezed the precious hydration past her burnt tongue and down her scratched-up throat. The cool liquid soothed tissues that had been screaming raw protest.

Only a little dribbling.

"I'm waiting."

Frankie took another sip, rubbing the jagged pins-and-needles feeling off her tongue.

"Orders," she finally croaked.

The woman tilted her head, one side of her mouth turning down, and waited. Clearly unimpressed. Her small, neat frame looked non-threatening. Probably never thrown a punch in her life. Then again, with her 'defensive aerosols,' she'd never need to.

Did she know about SystA? About Bruce? What could Frankie really tell her?

Nothing.

Frankie had used up her bulb. She considered shuffling over to grab another one. Maybe, in a minute.

The woman sighed. "Well, you're not pirates. Mercenaries? Trackers?"

"Cargo crew."

"Sure you are."

Suddenly, the water Frankie had just drunk threatened to come back up, with force. She swallowed hard. Reminded herself to breathe.

"Call your ship," the woman said.

Okay. "Ship...?" Frankie rasped toward the discreet speaker grill in the ceiling.

"Captain," Ship's voice projected strongly—stern. Anxious? "You've been contaminated. Immediate full shower required."

The woman looked toward the speaker. "Bossy."

Took one to know one.

Frankie tried to say "thanks" but her "th" wouldn't work. She settled for "'Kay."

"Remove boots immediately," Ship insisted. "Place in sterile field box, to your left, with the lights on. Proceed directly to shower—fully clothed. Water rinse."

Their "guest" sighed. "She's not going anywhere until I get my luggage. Bright green cases—you can't miss them." Honey pleasant, steel sharp.

Ship didn't respond.

"Ship?" Frankie said.

"Fine," Ship said. "Two minutes, Captain. Try not to move."

Frankie slowly pulled a knee up, slowly bent forward. Her mitten-fingers stumbled trying to release her boot straps.

Two minutes never took so long.

At last, the double doors hissed open sharply, tucking themselves into the walls. A stack of three big green suitcases stood right at the door.

A pause, as if Ship thought this woman would go for that. Turn her back on Frankie.

Right.

The suitcases started to fly. They bounced roughly into the room's center. Booted by one of the larger spider bots, which quickly scurried out of view. The outer spacer suit and its helmet flew in shortly after. The helmet bounced off one of the cases and nearly hit the woman as she sat on the bed.

"Rude," the woman said.

The bigger bot stayed in the hall, but one of the littler spiders scuttled in. It held aloft an oddly lumpy pillowcase. It scooted past the woman, past Frankie, toward the back shower annex.

"Captain," Ship repeated with razor-edged patience. "Go. Shower now."

Frankie moved to rise, but her balance didn't seem up to it yet.

"Shouldn't ... our guest go first? She's been the most exposed."

The woman waved her free hand in unconcern. "Unnecessary. I'm immune. I did create the toxin, after all."

"Drink more water," Ship said, insistent. "Now. Then go."

Frankie didn't know how she managed it. The boots, especially. But she was in the shower, the steamy water soaking blissfully into her skin. Her lungs gradually surrendered their shredded feeling. The gentle pulsing warmth eased away layers of tension and pain.

The icky lilac-scented soap assaulted her senses, though. She'd forgotten to trade it out for the unscented kind she preferred. But it was kind of a relief to know her sense of smell was online enough to tell the difference.

Frankie reentered the medical suite a half-hour later, wearing the outfit Ship and the little spider had delivered. Black tactical gear, including new reinforced grav-boots. She'd had never seen any of it before. Ship must have printed it out fresh. The pillow case also had contained a couple of Frankie's favorite protein bars —the mint ones.

She felt steadier now, but no wiser. Her wary gaze immediately returned to their "guest."

The woman was in the same spot, sitting cross-legged on the far bed, but her luggage had been moved closer to the bed. The cases weren't open, though, and she was still wearing her spacer undersuit. A small medical scanner rested in her lap, maybe to check the air quality?

"Better?" the woman said.

Frankie sat on the other bed. The snacks she'd left out were gone. Maybe she should just lie down here and take a nap.

Yeah, no.

"Not ... bad," she said.

"Delightful. Let's try this again," the woman said. "Spill."

Frankie rubbed still-tingly fingers through her short hair.

"Galactic Patrol delivered you to us. They never opened the outer capsule."

The woman's laugh could cut diamonds. "Try harder."

"SystA?"

"We're not sisters. Wait." The woman tapped her knee, thinking. "Small spiders bite?"

"Itsy bitsy spider bites."

The dark-haired stranger visibly relaxed. Turned out she had a long, graceful neck. "Then it worked."

Frankie did not feel as relieved as she might have. Poisoning her was part of the plan? Picked a lovely ally, Bruce.

"Right. I'm Prakara Gold." The woman paused, expecting Frankie to recognize the name. At Frankie's blank look, she went on. "You really are a cargo hauler, aren't you? I'm only the most brilliant physicist of our age." She posed, shoulders back, as if for a portrait. "According to Physics Today, NewsSum, and the Regent of the Cooperative Realm herself."

The woman came with her own citations.

"Okay," Frankie said, not bothering to look impressed. She had a citation from the regent herself. For all the good that did.

"So where are we exactly? Your stupid computer denied map access. Any access, really."

No surprise. Ship didn't like being called stupid, or a computer.

"So," Prakara Gold said. "How far are we from Base Twelve?"

Frankie looked toward the speaker in the ceiling.

"Eight hours from Base Twelve," Ship, sharp, from the speaker. Not even hiding the fact that there were cameras in this room.

Prakara Gold smiled veiled satisfaction. "Perfect. The patch will easily last that long." She touched the skin behind her right ear. Anti-nausea meds. "So. Get along with you now, and find me something real to eat." She waved her left hand toward the door.

"Got any more surprises?" Frankie said. "Any other 'defensive measures' we should prepare for?"

"Oh, captain. Let's not play that game, shall we?" Prakara Gold leaned toward Frankie, eyes wide like Frankie was a particularly interesting bug. she reached into a pocked and pulled out a small silver cylinder. More poison? She clicked it theatrically, showing it was spent, and tossed it toward the recycler. It bounced off and landed on the floor instead.

"There. All out of tricks. For now." She waved her hand dismissively. "Now go find us something to eat, while I make sure the facts are still what they were when I went to sleep."

Frankie was not reassured. Probably more 'defensive aerosols'—and who knew what else—in all that green luggage.

But Frankie had weapons, too.

And Prakara Gold had no idea.

CHAPTER
SEVEN

THE KITCHEN SMELLED HEAVENLY. Wave after wave of simmered turmeric mingled with hints of cumin, chased by the rich, buttery breath of slow-cooked vegetables. Frankie inhaled deeply, grateful that her sense of smell was back fully online after that fiasco in the medical bay.

She had excavated the very last batch of Beth's aloo gobi from the deepest corner of the freezer. She deserved it, for not dying of mystery toxin. Her friend had packaged a dozen generous portions—delightful treasures cuddled into insulated containers and a blanket of industrial-grade wrap, protected further by that now-beloved sunshiny duvet. They had survived the long, precarious passage on four ships and five station-transfers before finally reaching Frankie on the Spear, mere days after her birthday.

Beth was a planner.

Frankie, well. It was seven months until her next birthday.

But she was feeding the best to guests. Her momma would be so proud.

Would have been.

Thinking of Beth was always a double-edged sword. Always the threat of falling down the memory well, and not being able to swim.

But curry wasn't a flavor back home. They'd learned to make it—and Beth, to perfect it—when they were on Zichi, the Cooperatives' capital planet. The dishes they made stood for success, and overcoming, and victory.

And love.

Frankie scooped herself out some of that curry goodness, and then set the lid on the pot. Actual simmering, not even flash-heating. Beth's curry was too good for that.

She brought the bowl to the table of her favorite cozy nook, the closest of the two U-shaped high-backed benches with orange upholstery ringing gray metal tables. The table already had utensils, six bulbs of water and one of ginger beer.

Frankie sat so she could see the doorway into the hall. Spike, who had been hovering tense and bristling against Frankie's thigh, jumped on the back of her bench and settled, tense and bristling, against her neck.

The cyvlossic—and four of the bigger spider bots—had been just outside the door to the medical suite when Frankie walked out. Her little army had followed Frankie down the hall, the bots peeling off one by one to take up stations along the wall. Sweet, but a little late.

The metal spoon clinked pleasantly against the sturdy pottery, steam curling upward in golden wisps. Frankie closed her eyes as her first bit melted on her tongue like sunlight. Sweet coconut whispering through soft-as-butter cauliflower; the gentle heat of ginger lifting layers of warm spices.

She sighed, swallowed, smiled, her eyes still closed.

"Bitch doesn't deserve it," Spike growled behind her. Frankie could hear the glare. Glad it wasn't directed at her.

She took another mouthful, and let it linger, before she answered.

"Be fair," she said mildly. "Prakara Gold came out of that pod an asshole, but we don't know she went in that way."

Spike snorted. Her tail flicked Frankie's ear.

"No. Pod travel sucks." Frankie stirred her bowl, breathing in the peppery brightness of the turmeric. "The curry will bring her around."

Another ear flick.

She'd almost finished her first bowl—wasn't going to lick it, when there were seconds available—when Prakara Gold swept regally into the galley. Literally swept, decked out in a vivid emerald-green sleeveless gown that rustled as she walked. Rings on her fingers and bangles along her arms glittered in the kitchen's warm light. Her hair was up, the thick braid pinned in a complicated pattern at the nape of her neck.

"You dressed for dinner?" Frankie asked, spoon hovering midair.

Gold didn't respond. Instead, she stepped up to the side of the the bench Frankie and Spike were occupying and shoved the cyvlossic hard. Spike, surprised, actually swayed.

And then growled.

"Shoo, fat kitty. People are eating."

Those were battle words.

Frankie stood up quickly, forcing Gold to take a step back, away from Spike. She didn't look at the cyvlossic. Let Gold be speared by that indignant glare.

"Have a seat," Frankie said to Gold, indicating the spot across the table from her. Away from Spike.

The woman better not ever go to sleep on this ship.

Spike held grudges.

"Your clumsy robots damaged my Sainte Devries luggage," Gold said, settling on the bench with a sweep of stiff silk. "Only case I could get open had my Central District wardrobe. Ridiculous."

Maybe Ship held grudges, too.

Prakara Gold waved down at the emerald bodice, embroidered with something that looked like twining vines. "Afternoon tea dress. Silk, of course."

That color would look great on the walls of the bedroom. Frankie had forgotten how jewel tones made everything pop—even her own bronze-skinned apple-shaped self. She'd had a dress like that, but softer, as a debutante. Wonder where it was now.

Gold reached for a water bulb, bangles jingling, and then looked at Frankie's empty bowl. She inhaled deeply, and her shoulders eased. "Any more of that?"

"Sure," Frankie said. She could almost see Spike plotting how to ruin the dress. Not her problem. "You like curry? My friend made it for my birthday."

"Fine," said Prakara Gold.

Frankie got another bowl. She scooped a half-portion for her guest and a full portion for herself.

Gold eyed the dish suspiciously as Frankie set it down "Yellow? Curry should be green."

"Curries come in many colors," she said, seating herself. "As you know, having attended events in the Central District."

Prakara Gold gave a long, exasperated sigh. "Got anything else?"

Frankie reached for the woman's bowl and brought it over to her own side. Beth's curry would be wasted on this woman. "Usual spacer fare. Help yourself."

"Seriously? What kind of ship is this?"

"Cargo ship. Your memory is going."

With a single exaggerated sigh, Gold stalked to the gray

fridge-freezer and pulled the freezer-side door open. Her jewelry made the movement sound like she was in a musical.

The most brilliant physicist of their age knew her way around a ship's galley. She set something that looked like macaroni and cheese to spin in the reheater and turned back to Frankie. She started to lean a hip against the gray galley counter, and then seemed to think better of it. Instead, she started to pace on the diagonal, from the reheater to the hallway door, and back again.

"This is the story," she said as she came closer to Frankie. "White Moon Landing is a research base. Officially, it's a toxic site because of an experiment gone bad. So the ships that go there can say they are doing remediation and cleanup."

She walked away, checked on her food. Still spinning. She returned to pacing.

"In actual fact, it's for the Co-op's favorite astrophysics geniuses—research too risky for civilized worlds."

Frankie, having inhaled her second bowl of curry, moved on to Prakara's. Getting poisoned apparently took a lot out of a spacer.

"So why aren't you there already?" she asked between bites.

Gold tugged the now-hot meal casually from the reheater— forgetting oven mitts entirely—and hissed briefly between clenched teeth before dropping the steaming bowl onto the table. She rubbed her singed fingers together a moment.

Frankie did not offer medical assistance.

Gold settled back onto the bench seat. The cheesy macaroni appeared pale and unappetizing—no hot sauce, or even black pepper—but she scooped a mouthful, chewing thoughtfully before speaking.

"Acceptable." She looked at Frankie. "Where do you think I did the research that won me fame and fortune? I spent ten years on that rock." Gold took another bite of the white-on-white noodle dish, and sighed in happiness.

"Great," Frankie said. "So now you're back."

"There's been some trouble." Gold set her spoon down, bracelets ringing, as if she'd just remembering that whatever it was should have made her lose her appetite. "Something's been stolen. Something important."

Frankie nested her now-empty bowls together. Hit the spot. She reached for another bulb of water, and grabbed the ginger ale, too.

"What could be worth all this skulking and freezing?" she said.

"A quantum dot sensor." Secret out, Gold picked up her spoon again and dug back in.

Frankie didn't get it. "Something that senses quantum dots?"

Gold groaned. "Let me simplify." She tapped her spoon against her teeth, thinking. "Part of the problem of getting quantum dots to interact is they can't sense one another. They don't communicate. So what if we found a way for one dot here to connect to another dot back on Zichi? Or any other planet."

Frankie twisted the ginger ale bulb open. "Okay. So, instantaneous communication?"

Prakara pointed the spoon at her. Frankie felt ridiculously pleased with herself.

"Imagine instantaneous communication or—even better—transportation. Like jump gates but portable. Possibly anywhere."

Frankie forgot the ginger ale bulb entirely. Recreating millennia-lost jump-gate technology would rock the Cooperative Realm to its core.

"You've recreated the jump-gate technology?"

"Maybe," Prakara Gold said. "Maybe not that big. Yet. But imagine: Shipping would be a breeze, once the connections were in place."

Frankie imagined she would be out of a job.

"But aren't quantum particles inherently unstable?" she asked.

"Details, details," Prakara Gold waved away one of the deepest conundrums in science. "It's still experimental, delicate. Dangerous. We must retrieve it immediately."

Frankie's stomach churned. Unstable jump-gate tech. A package could be delivered inside a person. A message could be used as a spear.

A whole planet could be destroyed.

Suddenly, Frankie couldn't breathe. Remembered panic roared back into her ears.

In a flash, Spike had dropped onto the bench right beside Frankie. Taking up space. Pushing her deeper into the booth.

Allowing her to put an arm around her warm, fuzzy, solid, safe self.

"Blech," sniffed Gold with distaste. "Unhygienic creatures. Why even keep one on ship?"

"Cargo ship," Frankie murmured into the whorl of black and gray at the top of Spike's head. "Keeps the mice down."

"Mice!" The woman's voice had range. "How can you even live like this?" She looked around. "Everything gray and dark. Or emergency orange."

Now they were talking. "What colors would you suggest?" Frankie leaned into Spike. "I'm thinking sky blue with gold trim. Or white?"

Prakara Gold looked at Frankie as if she were a paint-splotched bug. "We're saving entire worlds, and you worry about paint?"

Frankie sighed faintly against Spike's shaggy fur. She rested her cheek on Spike's forehead, heard the unvoiced growl. What a look the cyvlossic must be giving their guest.

"By going to the one place where we know the quantum-sensor-thingie isn't anymore?"

Gold's laugh could cut diamonds. "Please. This is investigation 101. I need to talk to the researchers. Find out how the theft occurred. There's fantastic security here. I need to know what kind of person could manage such a feat."

Okay, now Frankie did feel dumb.

Prakara Gold plowed on. "Your friends at Systems Analysis called you the best. Frankly, I have my doubts. But you do have a ship, and some kind of brain. We'll find a use for you." She reached for another bulb of water.

"Seven hours to White Moon Landing," Ship said into the silence.

CHAPTER
EIGHT

"IT'S LIKE THIS," Prakara Gold said, in a voice that dripped with "you'll never know as much as me" sauce. Frankie knew that tone well—her university professors had practically bathed in it. The Central District higher-ups, too.

Frankie was utterly immune.

Spike, however, looked like she might leap the table and sink jagged fangs into Gold's elegant neck.

Frankie slid a discreet hand through the lush tangle of the cyvlossic's fur, and gently tugged Spike closer on the orange-cushioned bench. Spike, seated, was tall enough that her whole wild-fuzzy head was above table-top height. She was big enough that she could not be pulled; she had to want to move.

She allowed herself to be drawn nearer until the comforting wall of heat that was her flank rested solidly against Frankie. Spike vibrated softly with barely contained menace, but Frankie relaxed slightly. Spike could still launch herself at the oh-so-brilliant scientist at any moment, but if Frankie threw herself at the cyvlossic she might be able to prevent complete disaster.

Possibly. Of course, the fact that doing something like that would mean sacrificing Frankie's health and wholeness was a consideration.

The mostly silver bracelets along Gold's arm jingled as she pulled up a floating screen above the table between them. Frankie made a mental note to apologize to Ship and the bots for her and ask politely for them to undo whatever they'd done to jam the rest of Gold's luggage shut. In that bleeding-edge style party dress, she looked like she was ready to open a ball or something.

Gold coaxed the screen expertly into three dimensions, transforming it into a luminous cube.

"Imagine the universe is a tapestry," Gold began, her rings catching the light as she manipulated the hologram. The display transformed into a shimmering fabric of interconnected points.

Spike started to grumble, low.

"Give her a chance," Frankie whispered.

"Most people think distance is absolute. That going from here"—she tapped a glowing node near her, then traced her finger slowly across the field to a sparkling node near Frankie—"to here requires physically passing through all points in between."

"Thus your sudden need for a ride," Frankie said.

Gold's answering smile was razor-thin. She rotated the luminous tapestry in the air. "True enough, for you and me. But not at the quantum level." She flicked her fingers and the image changed.

Now the two pulsing orbs, connected by a faintly shimmering threat of silver, blinked in synchrony. "Quantum particles, when entangled, remain connected no matter the physical distance. What affects one instantly affects the other."

"Like entanglement communication relays," Frankie nodded. "Expensive, limited to data streams, and prone to collapse under observation."

Gold paused, clearly caught off guard by Frankie's understanding. "Precisely," she conceded, slightly warmer now. "But we've advanced this principle far beyond mere communications."

The shimmering hologram returned to quiet normal space, stars and bigger planets only. Two glowing cube-shapes appeared, a twisting tunnel of energy looping unnaturally between them, its multidimensional curves dizzying to gaze upon. Frankie swallowed, eyes tracking its impossible geometry.

"We've developed a quantum synchronization chamber," God said. "We call it a coherence bubble. An object placed here"—a tiny ivory-white box appeared inside one of the glowing cubes—"is deconstructed down to the quantum level. Its quantum signature instantly 'reappears' here"—the box flickered and reformed neatly inside the second glowing cube.

"Wait." Frankie's heart raced, trying to get enough oxygen to her brain to figure this out. Or maybe because of what it meant. "You're… copying the object. That breaks no-cloning—"

"Not copying," Gold interrupted. "Transferring. The original is deconstructed at the quantum level, travels in a blink, and then is re-created at the destination. No duplicates reman."

Spike issued a hiss so sharp Frankie nearly jumped.

"Impossible," Frankie whispered. "The energy requirements alone—"

"Immense," Gold conceded. "Each blink expends power matching the monthly usage of a small moon. Currently, the field lasts one-eighth of a second. But it's stable enough to handle nanoparticles."

Frankie's mind raced through the implications. A chill ran down her spine. "If this succeeds—"

"Instantaneous shipping. No more jump gates. No Skolls monopolizing trade paths." Gold offered a too-thin, calculated smile directly at Frankie. "Think of it."

Frankie thought. Her own ship, the Spear, suddenly obsolete, irrelevant. Distance erased as easily as brushing crumbs off a table.

Where people could step from one world to another in an instant.

Or where weapons could be deployed anywhere, instantly.

Frankie sat back in the booth. This was dream-talk. Had to be.

Prakara Gold's smile grew wider, colder, more satisfied.

"But we're in very early stages. Experimental. The coherence nodes must be carefully chilled, fed enormous, consistent energies—almost an Orr's-box-worth per test run."

Both Frankie and Spike flinched at "Orr." Gold did not notice. Frankie sent that bit of Orr data straight to the dark room in her mind where she kept memories and details on Konrad Orr. And then she slammed that door.

"They've only successfully sent nanoparticles, so far, if my data is current." Gold tapped her chin, thinking. "Nanobots— molecular machines—were planned next."

Frankie crossed her arms, gripping her elbows. "Sounds… risky." Impossible. Terrifying. "What if something interrupts transfer?"

"Safety protocols are crucial, of course," Gold said, waving a jingling hand. "Multiple redundancy, failsafes built beneath failsafes. At the first hint of disruption, transmission reverses itself instantly."

But wasn't transmission itself instant?

Frankie's grip on her elbows tightened.

This was a galaxy-changing discovery.

If true.

Frankie leaned back, telling her pulse to slow. "Then what's your emergency? Someone steal your blueprints?"

"Worse." Gold's dark eyes hardened. She manipulated the holoscreen, inserting a dark third node that intercepted the connection path between the glowing cubes. "Our last transmission to Central was sabotaged. Someone replaced our data feed with garbage, making it look like the system itself failed catastrophically."

"Quantum data signals can be hacked?" Frankie couldn't picture how that would be possible. Then again, she was having trouble picturing quantum data signals acting like magic.

Gold's expression shuttered—pride mixed with resignation. "We didn't think so. And we're past mere data transmission anyway. This was a nanoparticle test, the second. The first, three weeks ago, went perfectly."

"But if someone falsified the feed—" Frankie began slowly.

"Exactly." Gold's fingers clenched, distorting the hologram. "That means someone has either developed technology beyond what we thought possible, or—"

"So you're not the smartest scientists in the system."

"Or we have a mole." Gold swiped the screen away so hard her bracelets clacked as well as jangled. "There are only three coherence boxes—one at White Moon Landing, one at a moon very near White Moon, and a final one at the Cooperative Space Capitol Complex on Zichi." The capital of the Cooperative Realm, four jump-gates away from here. Scientists were nothing if not ambitious.

"The boxes are locked down, of course" Gold said. "Only six people have clearance. But the control systems..." She shrugged. "Perhaps they could be hacked by someone close to one of the boxes. That's what the corresponding scientist on White Moon Landing thinks."

"Control systems? Like maintenance?"

"Or communications. Anyone on the base with the right skills could potentially access those."

Frankie looked up, at the speaker where Ship was surely listening in. "You think someone on White Moon Landing hacked the transmission?"

"It's the logical answer. To cut into the receiving end would be impossible. More impossible."

This whole thing was impossible.

"We have a highly placed traitor, someone capable enough to break our encryption utterly," Gold finished bitterly. She sighed, glancing distractedly toward the dirty pans, the now-empty curry pan, beside the dishwasher.

A sudden longing for Beth washed across Frankie's heart. She should've taken the time to see her friend last month. Then she'd be on the way back from Zichi now, not about to orbit some mystery deadly space laser moon.

This wasn't a job for her.

"What exactly does Bruce think I can do about this?" Frankie demanded softly, finally asking the question that had been clawing at her. "I'm no physicist."

Gold shrugged, her pendant earrings jingling dramatically. "Bruce insisted you're the best." Her tone said otherwise.

Frankie swallowed her discomfort. Then Spike's heavy flank bumped her hip again.

Right.

Of course.

Frankie looked down at Spike, who was looking back at her like she was dense as triple-folded space.

Right.

Spike was the expert.

Her advanced cyber instincts and infiltration skills unmatched, Spike had saved their hides during the flight from the Skoll's warship. She knew how to get in and out of locked spaces, including safes, and finding escape routes.

She'd solve the puzzle. Frankie would finger the culprit.

Frankie let go of her elbows, realizing that they had been protesting their treatment for long minutes.

"Well?" Gold prompted aggressively. "What's your brilliant plan, detective?"

Frankie raised eyebrows at Spike. Spike blinked innocent, round eyes *Me? Just a scruffy monster kitty cat!*

As if.

Frankie pushed gently at Spike, who took the hint and hopped off the bench. Frankie slipped out of the nook, sweeping up the curry bowls and macaroni bowl.

"Give us just a minute, would you?"

STILL SEATED in the nook in the Spear's kitchen, Prakara Gold huffed in exasperation, jewelry chiming reproachfully, but made no move to follow as Frankie led Spike toward the hall. The cyvlossic's claws clicked confidently against the brushed-metal flooring, their sound synching with Frankie's rebounding pulse.

Frankie's her gallant little bot army still ranged along the walls between the kitchen and the infirmary, still standing like silent sentinels. Their array of reflective lenses tracked Frankie's steps, their little spider- or crab- or wheeled-feet clicked acknowledgement against the metal plating. Frankie smiled in gratitude, and turned away toward the pilot's room. Spike ignored the bots entirely, her fur even more ruffed, her shoulders tense beneath the tangle of black and gray fur.

The corridor's soft grays annoyed Frankie now. And all those hideous orange hand-holds, at top and bottom of every door frame, for when the ship lost gravity.

And the air recyclers were too loud.

Halfway between the kitchen and the pilot's room—should be far enough that Gold couldn't overhear—she stopped and turned back to the cyvlossic. Spike's fur may have been turbulent, but her eyes were calm.

"So, what's the plan?" Frankie said.

Spike didn't break stride. She brushed Frankie's thigh with her shaggy flank, more in disdain than affection. Her gaze flicked upward in a look of cool assessment that said only amateurs discuss secret missions in open hallways. Frankie groaned a sigh.

Fine.

She followed Spike into the pilot's room at the corridor's end, her steps heavy, her mind tangled. Once inside, the little semi-circle of a room wrapped snugly around her, the overhead glow a warmly reassuring gold. The two active monitor screens and the console pulsed in happy greens and blues. Nothing wrong here.

But Frankie didn't exactly settle into the wide comfortable pilot's chair on the left; dropping down hard enough to release air from its black leather-like padding was less like dignified sitting and more like flouncing.

She hated feeling so out of her league.

Spike pushed the lower door panel. The inset door panel balked, and then slid shut.

So. Privacy.

Frankie pulled her legs up on the solidly padded seat and wrapped her arms around her shins.

Spike launched herself onto the matching pilot's seat next to her—tufts of stray gray and black catching in the light on their way to muck up the nav boards again.

The workstation spread comfortably wide, covered by logical arrays of buttons, toggles, two sturdy backup joysticks, touch-pads, and two "universal" keyboards. Spike stepped onto the console that was part of the controls of the ship. She prowled over to the lower left visual panel controls and out came those pawpad-finger things.

Frankie looked away, back at the two cylindrical escape pods that flanked the door. Wondered if they had cryo functions. Decided not to look.

Easily one-quarter of Spike was reinforced cybernetic tech. Eyes that scanned everything, including her own incoming messages. Memory vault-deep. Able to withstand a minute or two in vacuum. Any creature less secure might have seemed monstrous. Spike somehow just became fascinating. If rude.

Frankie still didn't know how Spikes mechanical larynx got scorched. She could get it fixed; SystA surely had offered. But she'd refused, Bruce said. She'll tell you someday, maybe.

"One," Spike rasped. "You're arm candy for this job."

Really rude.

"Distract the humans. I'll talk to the machines."

Spike tapped the control pad for the monitor, running through menus in some other language. A lineup of photos of people's heads popped onto the screen. Two rows of three people. The images were taken in the same bland gray location, and no one looked like they were enjoying the experience. First day on the job shots.

"Suspects," Spike said.

"We're sure it's an inside job?" Frankie tingled at the phrase "inside job." For a second she felt like she was in one of those caper shows. Then Spike gave her a look.

"Impossible not," she said. "Other two collection spots, moon and Zichi, are bot-run."

Frankie frowned at Spike. "A bot could pull it off. Ship could do it. Couldn't you Ship?"

"Perhaps," Ship said, from the console speakers, her honeyed voice almost a drawl. "If sufficiently motivated."

"I knew you were listening!"

Ship did not respond to that. Instead, she said, "Prakara Gold is drinking the last orange drink."

"What? How did she find it?" The bulb of Rosing's Orange

Tasty was tucked back behind all the other drinks, waiting for an emergency or a celebration. Or until they could restock at their home base, Rosing Station. "She's digging through our stuff?"

Spike almost hissed. "Focus," she rasped, eyes narrowed.

Right. Frankie shook herself mentally and leaned forward, focusing squarely on the faces on the screen. "Fine. So say I get all these people in the same room. Then what?"

"Study, listen, divert attention."

That sort of sounded like a plan. "Giving you time to break into their systems. How long do you need?"

Spike tilted her head, thinking. "First chunk will take some time. After that, shorter. Patterns easier."

Frankie considered carefully. She stretched her legs down, feet touching the floor.

"They are not going to let you anywhere near the tech."

Spike drew back, fur bristling. "Companion animal," the cyvlossic said. Their go-to lie; one that allowed Spike access nearly everywhere.

"Companion?" Frankie eyes the thick stray wisps of fur on Spike's chair. "More likely biohazard. Are you molting?"

Spike's ears flattened. "Seasonal."

"So," Frankie said. "Definitely need a spa day."

FRANKIE STARED. If she hadn't watched the entire spa session herself, she might not have recognized the sleek creature now standing sullenly in front of her.

Gone was the walking dust-mop that had been shooting fur everywhere. In its place stood a gleaming, streamlined being whose graceful curves more closely resembled a sleek, wet river otter than a ship-bound cyvlossic. Her striking striped coat lay smooth and radiant, reflecting the greenhouse room's bright glow lights in waves of polished charcoal trimmed with faint high-lights of gray—and a hint of burnt orange. Intricate stripes hugged muscled shoulders and flowed across her powerful flanks.

"That's the real you?" Frankie asked softly, circling Spike in slow, amazed steps. The greenhouse's typically mild scent of humid mint and tomato vines was now interwoven with the lingering fragrance from the depleted tins of HairBHaiv gel, the beloved styling cream Frankie had been hoarding for herself. Bad news for Frankie's own styling options this trip.

Four hours of careful grooming, relentless brushing, and very patient handling—mostly done by the spider bots, thank the stars —had left the corner of the room that had gardening implements carpeted in discarded cyvlossic fur. Frankie was pretty sure enough fluff lay scattered across the clay tiles to construct another full Spike entirely.

Maybe the little bots could use it as stuffing for pillows. Or braid the hair. Or make a fake Spike, who smiled.

Spike's amber eyes narrowed to skeptical, familiar slits. Yeah, it was still her in there.

Spike had endured the exhaustive grooming marathon—even the water-rinsing parts—with admirable (if growling) stoicism. Only twice had she swiped warning at the intrepid trio of diligent helper bots. Frankie had managed the spraying and the mopping up, tasks that kept her away from any claws.

"May I?" Frankie asked, hovering one hand cautiously over Spike's now-silky head.

Spike flicked newly tamed ears—stunningly outlined with that black-fur edge—and grudgingly nodded.

Frankie's fingers sank into sumptuousness, fur soft and dense as fine velvet. "Like warm silk," she said. "You're incredible."

One of the bots displayed its front camera view so Spike could see. She studied the image, tilting her head from side to side, then stretched, testing how her new coat moved with her body. The dismissive tail flick that followed suggested gruff approval.

"Still… me?" came Spike's scratchy voice from the mechanism near her neck. Nothing they could do about that.

"Absolutely still you," Frankie said. "In the shape of a no-shed companion animal, perfect for science facility access."

"Better?" Spike asked, amber eyes unblinking.

"For the mission? Definitely," Frankie said. "For scaring the pants off scared and suspicious scientists? We'll see."

Spike's mouth opened slightly in what might have been a smile.

"Still bite," she said.

***

WHITE MOON LANDING WAS A LIE.

For starters, its lumpy, misshapen orb was the same feature-less dull gray as every forgettable second-rate moon Frankie had seen across who knew how many systems.

Secondly—and this was the kicker—ships didn't even land on the place.

Instead, the Spear hovered silently in the fierce, color-draining glare of the system's dwarf star, patiently awaiting the arrival of the moon's bizarre protrusion—an elevator shaft shaped like a blunt, battered steel pier. The really very flimsy looking thing slowly rotated toward them as Ship got into position. Apparently ships stuck their noses gingerly into the open end of this tube and sneezed their passengers out.

Fantastic.

But White Moon Landing would really rather that nobody bother. Since the Spear had come in close range, the landing's communications array had blared emergency sirens and blasted klaxon-loud messages that all had the same meaning: Visitors Not Welcome. Do not Even Think About Landing Here.

A message that had not changed as they neared. Or when they hailed the station on every channel. Or now, when Frankie and Prakara Gold waited in the cold tippy-tip of the first sphere of the Spear, getting ready to inject themselves into the elevator tunnel. The tunnel whose lights blinked warning ambers and reds.

"You're sure about this?" Frankie muttered through clenched teeth. She and Prakara Gold were both in full spacer gear—Prakara's pristine ensemble next to Frankie's scuffed, practical vacuum gear. Their helmets were off, for now, the icy cabin air pinching painfully at Frankie's ears. The tip of her nose was going numb.

The two waited in the cramped, freezing tip of the Spear's smallest bulb, the top sphere of its snowman-like, three-sphere design. The practical but uncomfortable for humans space dedicated to engines, gravity manipulation equipment, and the power management hardware. Around them, tightly bundled insulated cables thrummed with suppressed thermal energy. Despite the ship's insulation, Frankie felt wave after wave of chill slap at her.

Gold flashed a confident smile—irritatingly cheerful. Beside her, one of Ship's sturdy crablike maintenance bots dutifully gripped the straps of Gold's trio of massive emerald-green luggage. Frankie's polite conversation with Ship and the bots earlier had convinced them to repair the bent latches—and confiscate another of those defensive toxin canisters—but Frankie was still waiting for a thank you from Gold. Frankie's own single, humble yellow canvas backpack sat lightly across her back.

She tried distracting herself by peering through the tiny frost-edged porthole beside the square double-door emergency airlock, watching the spit-and-chewing-gum-style elevator shaft inching relentlessly their way.

"Warning says once we step out down there, all our skin will melt off."

"They wish," Gold said, flicking her immaculately gloved hand in dismissal. "Standard scare tactics. If they really thought we were a danger, they would have grav-blasted us into the orbit of the sun." At Frankie's blank look of shock, Gold smirked. "No evidence to clean up afterwards."

Gold was all perky happiness now. No doubt everyone at White Moon Landing knew exactly who the brilliant Dr. Prakara Gold was and they were prepared to fawn accordingly.

Better them than her.

Meanwhile, Spike floated alongside her inside a mostly transparent large animal transit box, seething. Cyvlossics, notoriously tough even when not enhanced, actually could handle vacuum briefly. How briefly, Frankie had no intention of ever finding out. But Spike's disguise as a companion animal meant the enclosure was mandatory.

Frankie hoped Gold wouldn't see Spike discreetly repositioning the enclosed box herself, shifting it imperceptibly by pawing a corner of the absurd fake pee-pad on the bottom. So embarrassing. Spike peed in the toilet, like everyone else.

"You look like a grumpy bullet," Frankie teased. Spike refused to even glance in her direction, but the large animal box floated farther away from her.

Outside the porthole, amid stark shadows and harsh highlights, White Moon Landing lay like a geometric bloom across the pockmarked lunar surface. At its heart, the broad central torus gleamed faintly pearl-gray beneath the relentless glare of the white dwarf star, shielded carefully beneath protective layers of lunar regolith and reflective materials. Surrounding it, smaller interconnected ring-shaped modules radiated outward, joined by short corridors that looked far too delicate from this height. A single extended corridor stretched outward, leading to the base of the elevator. No visible movement, no welcoming committee on the surface. Emphatically, nobody outside.

Frankie swallowed tightly. She slipped her helmet on.

"Ship?" She flicked her helmet's comm to their private secure channel, hearing Spike softly joining with a reassuring pop.

Calm and reassuring, Ship's voice purred gently through her earpiece. "Systems remain friendly. AI colleagues very chatty."

Of course. The AIs and bots chatted away at one another, even when humans kept stubbornly silent. "What do they say?"

Ship filled her in. Close to a hundred people on a base built for four hundred. Plenty of food. Military-style organization. Talk to the Chief of Staff first, not the Lead Scientist.

Panic in the halls after the quantum dot sensor disappeared.

Sadly, the Moon's friendly non-human crew could not shed much light on what had happened to the sensor. That wing of the research area was under its own AI and firewalled to a fare-thee-well.

She caught Spike's eye. The cyvlossic gave her a nearly imperceptible nod.

Head there first.

At last, the elevator shaft swung near enough that Spear nosed in. Its mouth yawned darkly in front of them, comms still ringing with threats, guiding lights still flashing amber and red.

But there was standard pressure inside the dark tube. And there was air, supposedly.

Whatever waited down there—experiment, prototype, tool, weapon—could rewrite their worlds. Trade routes, jump gates, governments. Even the boundaries of possibility.

And someone who had managed to sneak into it.

Someone they needed to find. And shut down.

Frankie pushed the panel to open both sets of airlock doors.

Time to dive in.

CHAPTER
ELEVEN

WHITE MOON LANDING'S entry sterilization cycle finished mercifully fast, happy sensors chiming softly. Frankie shook off the lingering tingle of electrostatic mist and sick-ozone air and straightened her favorite cobalt blue tunic—with pockets!—as she stepped into the cool, polished silence of the base itself.

Or rather, a long arched corridor broken up by the kind of emergency doors that slam down from the top. She'd seen the doors from the elevator shaft, square slabs of scary metal looking precariously balanced out there in the vacuum, set on the top of the arch like an invading army ready to pounce. Most of the corridors had the slide-from-the-side doors, but this one and one leading out to a single, lonely donut building had these old-fashioned, hardcore ones.

The corridor's gently curved walls were new-style, though, that bone-pale material that reminded Frankie of the smooth interior surface of an enormous porcelain shell. No windows, and nothing stuck to it. Relentlessly minimal.

Frankie had expected a greeting party—or at least someone to acknowledge their arrival. They hadn't been subtle about it.

Nobody.

Spike padded silently at her heels. Frankie was still getting used to the new, sleek Spike. Less like an oversized dust mop and more like a tiger shark. Her tufted ears swiveled, catching sounds too faint for stupid humans to hear. Frankie was a little bit afraid to brush up against the cyvlossic—what if a single too-electro-static touch made all that fur go wild again?

Five entire minutes later, Prakara Gold emerged, leading a wheeled minicart stacked with her massive emerald suitcases.

"You're sure this is the right place?" Frankie said. The too-quiet, spare corridor reminded her of a freighter she'd once explored after its crew had mysteriously abandoned it. That hadn't ended well—she still had a scar on her left shoulder from the encounter. Should have asked Ship to scan the place for monsters.

Gold tossed her perfectly coiffed hair, the braid wrapped around her head like crown. Her emerald two-piece pantsuit shushed with each step. Apparently determined to make an impression.

"We must have been a surprise," she said, shushing past Frankie, headed toward the base itself.

Right.

Frankie shook her wristcom to wake it up, and sent a query to Ship.

"Won't work," Gold said.

She was right. The wristcom screen went red-text: No connection.

"Communications are secured to base-only, except in the main office," Gold said. "Quite restful."

Spike's ears flicked forward, toward the base, and held.

A woman rounded the corner at the far end of the hall. She made a standard spacer undersuit with a black labcoat over top look beautiful, the fabric flowing around her tall frame as she moved with swift purpose. Her henna-red hair was pulled back with an emerald headband, though a few strands had escaped to frame her face.

Chief of Staff Scarletti Bulwarion. Her first-day-at-work photo didn't do her justice.

Just ahead of Frankie, Prakara Gold went completely still. Interesting.

The woman met them where they were.

"Professor Gold," she said, her alto voice crisp and professionally neutral. "Imagine seeing you here again." Her gaze swept over Frankie and lingered on Spike, one hennaed eyebrow raising slightly.

Gold lifted her sharp chin slightly, shoulders going rigid as if bracing for impact.

"Scarlett," she said coolly after a fractional pause. Her bangles jangled as she put a hand on her chest, noticed what she was doing, and pressed the hand down, as if smoothing a wrinkle from the pristine suit. "Still chief of staff, I see."

The woman's gaze lingered just a second too long for comfort before shifting to Frankie.

"Chief of Staff Scarletti Bulwarion," she said, extending a hand to Frankie. Her grip was firm, her skin cool and dry. "Call me Scarlett."

"Frankie Styles. And this is Spike, my special companion."

Scarlett's nostrils flared slightly as she bent to examine Spike more closely. "Companion animal. What is it? House cat had a run-in with a tiger?"

Spike glared back, unblinking, her amber eyes fixed on Scarlett with an intensity that made the chief of staff straighten up fast.

"Spike is special," Frankie said. "Aren't you, Spikey?"

Spike's tail twitched once—a controlled motion that Frankie

recognized as restraint rather than irritation. The promised payback would come later.

Scarlett recovered quickly, though she took a step back from Spike. "Never seen anything quite like it."

Her focus snapped back to Gold. "We weren't informed that you'd be coming personally, Professor," she said, voice calm but a flicker of tension at the corners of her eyes. "Central District was vague."

Gold carried her tension in that cut-glass jaw. "Classified," she said. "To avoid intercept."

Interesting.

Scarlett's soft exhale was almost masked by her pivot to face toward the main base. "Then let's start the tour. You're familiar with basic on-base safety, yes?"

"Yes," Frankie answered for all of them.

"Good. White Moon Landing is a modular base, using the torus model. Most of the living areas and labs are plain donuts, with open—quote-unquote, they're covered by a triple-thick window—centers for light, plantings, recreation, etcetera. The maintenance and storage areas are mostly jelly donuts, to give us the most possible space and flexibility."

Scarlett had a long stride. Frankie had to almost skip to keep up. She caught Gold watching Scarlett's back with an intensity that startled her. When Gold noticed Frankie watching, she quickly shifted her gaze to the plain walls around them.

Scarlett's patter was well practiced. "Our central ring—called the Commons—is where all main functions connect. Dining hall, meeting rooms, Command and Medical. Labs extend North and South, and cluster by research domain. Living quarters branch East and West."

Spike fell behind, sniffing what looked like a hidden door. Frankie looked at the corridor again. It wasn't completely rounded. Crew probably used the space for cables and whatever else. Everybody on the maintenance crew must be short and skinny.

"Cargo bays and mechanicals—and the elevator—sit further out along the perimeter, keeping the noise and bustle down for the scientists," Scarlett said. Pain in the butt for the supply workers, though. Even if they were mostly bots. "And a single semi-detached ring, our Hazard Lab, sits the farthest out. Fully shielded with independent environmental and security management. Right now it's the quantum lab."

Finally, a wide double sliding door appeared at the end of the corridor. The central ring. But Scarlett stopped just a few steps away from it.

"We'll take the underground way." she said, gesturing toward another of those almost hidden doors. She placed an elegant, bare hand on the control panel, hesitating a fraction of a second before entering the code.

This one opened onto a shallow gray ramp lined with mini-cart tire marks. "This is how we bring in all our dot-scientists," Scarlett said.

"We know all that," Prakara Gold said, her heels clicking sharply against the floor.

"No we don't," Frankie shot back. "Not all of us."

Gold rolled her eyes. "Fine. Waste all our time."

Scarlett stopped halfway through the doorway. Her cool gaze locked on Gold.

"Of course, professor. Don't let us hold you back." She gestured toward the far end of the corridor they were in. "You do know the way."

Gold reacted as if she'd been slapped. She glanced down the hall. Frankie could've sworn the scientist shivered.

But if she did, she didn't let it change her tone. "Nonsense," she said. "Carry on."

Scarlett half-smiled as she turned back toward the ramp. Once through the doorway, she stepped aside to let the others enter, and then slid the door closed and locked it.

The square-walled tunnel, lit by long skinny white-light panels at hip height and directly overhead, smelled of minicart axle oil and moon dust. Warm, and not dusty at all. The floor must be polished rock.

Scarlett swept past them to take the lead. Against the black of her labcoat, her shoulder-length hair glowed like a beacon. Luckily, since her stride had her halfway down the ramp in a matter of seconds.

"The dotties are supposed to stay sequestered, but we can't really enforce that," she said, casting her voice back. "They have separate social areas and apartments, and supposedly a separate dining room, but it's really just the backside of the main dining room. So," Scarlett shrugged, "some mixing."

Prakara Gold's quick staccato steps sounded like a stilt walker chasing a seal. "Is that how the thief broke in?"

"TBD," Scarlett said. "Right?"

The corridor widened as they approached a junction, the ceiling rising to accommodate a series of pipes and conduits. Frankie could feel a subtle vibration through the soles of her boots—power systems, life support, the constant hum of a facility keeping humans alive in an environment designed to kill them.

"Surprised to see you here again," Scarlett said softly to Gold as they walked. "Sanders was too busy?"

Gold snorted. "Too fond of his acolytes."

"Mentees, they call them. Insurance for the future."

"Crutches," Gold said. "I didn't have a mentor."

"And you don't take mentees."

"What's that supposed to mean?"

As they passed through the first of three security checkpoints, Frankie noted the thickness of the doors— reinforced metal at least a hand's width wide—and the redundant locking mechanisms. Whatever they were protecting here, they were serious about keeping it contained.

Or keeping others out.

At the third door, Scarlett noticed Frankie's interest. "I use this route to try to scare some sense into these head-in-the-clouds thinkers."

"Does it work?" Frankie asked.

"Mostly."

Spike padded alongside, occasionally brushing against Frankie's leg. Without her usual cloud of fur, the contact felt different—more deliberate, a silent signal between them. Something about this place had her on edge, too.

The security doors each required Scarlett's palm print and retinal scan. The temperature dropped noticeably with each threshold they crossed, until Frankie could see her breath forming small clouds in front of her face.

"You'll find much as you left it, Professor Gold," Scarlett said as they approached the ramp to the final door. "This donut is new, yes, but it's the same layout as the older one." She waited for the door to slide open with a pneumatic hiss. "Except for this."

Frankie felt a cold shiver that had nothing to do with the room's temperature.

CHAPTER
TWELVE

FRANKIE FOUGHT the urge to hold her breath as the quantum lab's final security door eased aside, the rush of chilled air from the room biting her cheeks

Stepping through, she stopped short, eyes wide. She'd anticipated a "standard" lab, with scientists bent over black resin tabletops, adjusting knobs on various pieces of equipment, with prototypes scattered about. Sinks and eyewash stations, and whiteboards covered in equations. But the quantum lab, nestled into the curved, hollowed rim of the torus, felt like stepping into a shuttle port traffic control room, mid-emergency.

Stark white walls curved slightly upwards to a gently rounded ceiling, lit brightly by recessed white illumination panels that cast no shadows. The lab must take up half of the plain donut-shaped building. She could see only a hint of the back wall around the curves of the sides. The floor grabbed gently at her boots, matte-black and rubberized, absorbing every stomp and step.

The room's sharp, ozone-laden scent was underscored by a metallic bitterness that lingered on her tongue like a copper coin.

Air scrubbers murmured constantly, cycling the chill and achingly dry air, crackling faintly with invisible static electricity. Frankie rubbed the goosebumps climbing her arms, painfully aware of each tiny hair standing up under her tunic.

Should've worn the long-sleeved undershirt.

Two long rows of adjustable desks—with familiar black resin countertops, at least—took up much of the space. The scientists worked with their backs to each other, a ring of floating screens in front of them with more, physical, screens propped on top of their tables. Anyone passing through the middle could see what everyone was working on.

The five scientists present did not fill the space. Each could have spread out to two more desks, if they'd wanted. But they were all clustered near the middle of the room. Bundled in heavy sweaters or thick cable-knit jumpers. One person had even retreated deeply within the hood of an oversized Angry Vibes sweatshirt, hands barely visible as he tapped on a tablet. They cast curious yet guarded glances toward Frankie and then, noticing Gold, quickly dropped their gazes to the monitors.

Spike padded alongside Frankie, her eyes scanning every person, every monitor screen, predatory. She drew a few startled glances from the scientists as they passed by, headed to the back of the room.

Scarlett swept steadily forward. At the far, curving end of the lab a clear wall, reinforced transparent aluminum, probably, cut the last little segment of the lab into a small chamber, like a supervisor's office. But all that was inside was a squat, square metal table, with a solid-looking gray metal cube as big as Spike on top. It looked like a high-end fabricator, boxes of various shapes and sizes that took various slurries of ingredients and made them into millions of things. Even food, but you didn't want to think about that too hard.

This one was different.

Isolated.

Important.

Scarlett keyed the security panel beside the inner chamber's door, near the inner wall of the torus. Her palm glowed briefly, and the door clicked, unlocked.

"Come inside," she said, voice low as if the cold quiet of this place required hushed reverence.

Frankie stepped forward, but Gold shoved briskly past her, forcing Spike to press tight against Frankie's thigh for balance. Frankie felt a growl building in the cyvlossic's chest but all that came out was a unvoiced hiss.

Inside the inner chamber, the ozone-metal intensified, rolling thickly against Frankie's tongue, cold enough that her lungs protested. The room felt pressurized in more ways than one, sharpening every sound and sensation.

"This is it." Scarlett approached the cube, placing a hand gently against its dull-gray side. "Our quantum transmitter. Anything placed inside—it disappears here and reappears over on the next moon or a star system away—instantly."

"Anything?" Frankie swallowed hard. Unbelievable.

But Scarlett believed.

"Well, anything smaller than a nanite, so far," Scarlett said. "But it was a micronanite last year!"

"We started with data packets," a clipped, nasal voice interjected. "Ninety-seven percent success rate."

A short, spider-thin woman with steel-stranded black hair scraped into a bun had followed them into the room. Deep-set eyes peered from behind green-rimmed AR glasses halfway down her nose. Her jewel-red tunic over practical black pants disappeared beneath a tan wool coat with more pockets than Frankie had seen on a single garment.

"Dr. Jin Wint," Scarlett said to Frankie. "Our lead quantum dynamics researcher. Frankie Styles," she said to Wint.

Wint barely spared Frankie a glance, laser-focused instead on Prakara Gold. Who, Frankie finally noticed, had gone silent since entering the lab.

"Prakara," Wint said, voice chilling. "An unexpected… pleasure. I wasn't aware your expertise would be required for this… situation."

"The regent wanted the best, Jin." Gold smiled with all the warmth of a predatory fish. "I'm sure you understand."

Wint's nostrils flared. "Naturally. Though I'm surprised you could tear yourself away from Central District. I heard your position at Science Archives was quite… prestigious."

Spike's ears perked forward. Frankie stepped closer to Scarlett, in case a fight broke out.

"Ninety-seven to the next moon," Prakara said, ignoring the jab and gesturing toward the quantum box. "Eighty-two percent success rate to Central District."

Wint tapped the side of her glasses. "Eighty-nine-point-nine now. We've made adjustments to the field stabilizers since your… departure."

"Impressive," Gold said in a tone that suggested the opposite.

Frankie cleared her throat, startling both of them. "So, one of these was stolen?"

"Not the device itself," Wint scoffed. "Obviously."

"Not stolen—intercepted," Scarlett clarified, tapping her wrist communicator. A translucent floating screen sprang into existence in front of her, long lines of equations scrolling across its face. She turned the screen to face Frankie, Gold, and Wint.

Frankie couldn't begin to read it, even when it was facing right. She must have looked like she felt, because Scarlett swiped the screen again. The numbers changed into a familiar image of planets and the gravitational waves that swept among them, and then the visual representation of space-time folding that Gold had shown them first in the kitchen of the Spear. Intricate gravitational dances cascading across simplified grids.

"We're folding space itself," Scarlet said, reverence back in her voice. "Where the edges touch, we can transmit dots."

"How are you folding the space, exactly?" Frankie asked.

"Classified," Scarlett and Wint answered simultaneously.

Of course.

"Okay," Frankie said. "So. A box at one edge can send an object to a box at the other edge."

"Not an object," Gold snapped. "A data packet."

"No," Wint countered. "We can do nanobots, now."

"Only to the next moon," Gold fired back.

"For now," Wint returned.

"Okay, great," Frankie said, using her foot to push a reluctant Spike between the two physicists. They transferred their glares to the cyvlossic. "So then, what happened?"

"Yes, Miss Scarlett," Gold said, still snappish. "Tell us what happened."

Before Scarlett could answer, a soft voice spoke from the still-open door.

"Chief?" A woman stood hesitantly by the doorway. Auburn curls held messily back, skin warm gold-brown, her practical brown overalls lightly smudged. The scents of rich soil and faint herbs slipped in among the stark metallic tang. "The, um, power allocation report?"

"Yes, Tala?" Scarlett said, her calm mask momentarily slipping with mild irritation.

"You said you wanted it right away. Right?" She lifted the data tablet in her hand defensively.

"Right." Scarlett held out her left hand. "Meet Tala Foss. Environmental Systems Engineer." She matched her photo, down to the curls spilling out of her scrunchie.

"I've highlighted the anomalies in the secondary cooling

power system," Foss said softly. She must have just come from the base's greenhouse. "There's a pattern to the—"

"Is that relevant?" Gold said. "We're discussing quantum field dynamics, not maintenance issues."

Foss didn't flinch, but for a slight tightening around her eyes. She continued addressing Scarlett. "Thirty-minute intervals, just under alert thresholds, multiple times, starting weeks ago…" Her voice grew firmer when she was talking data.

Wint waved dismissively. "Environmental systems are always fluctuating. That's hardly—"

"These aren't random," Foss insisted. "They're deliberate. Precisely calibrated to stay just below the automatic alert threshold."

Deliberate.

Sabotage.

Spike moved closer to Scarlett as she took the tablet. Cyvlossics had three kinds of wireless interfaces, at least. One could grab that data, surely. Then Spike scowled. The data must be encrypted.

"Thank you, Tala," Scarlett said. "I'll review this immediately."

Foss nodded and turned back toward the door. But before she could exit, a man blocked her way, hurrying into the room.

Mid-sized, very pale, with a meticulously trimmed copper-colored beard, carefully tousled hair, and expensive neural-link implants visible at his temples, the man took Foss's shoulder and pushed her to the side without taking his gaze off Gold.

His high-business attire—cream tailored shirt with a corporate-style knit vest in muted gray under a burgundy feltlike jacket seemed entirely out of place in the lab's icy austerity. Cedar-infused cologne rolled faintly after him, discordantly luxurious.

"Professor Gold!" His resonant voice filled the room. "Huxley Parker, Communications." He seized Gold's reluctant hand eagerly, oblivious or indifferent to her subtle recoil. "I've read all your papers on quantum entanglement stabilization. Your theory on cross-phase harmonization revolutionized the field."

"Yes," Gold said, extracting her hand.

In his other hand, Parker held his own data tablet. He thrust it toward Wint.

"Found something interesting in the sub-band ranges.," he said. "A recurring pattern that doesn't match our protocols."

Wint grabbed the tablet. Instantly Gold was at her shoulder, arguing about what it meant. Within moments, they'd fallen deep into rapid-fire technical jargon—an absolute wall of expertise.

Frankie carefully separated herself, and approached the more approachable Foss.

"Doctor?" Tell more about these power anomalies?"

"Really?" Foss blinked in surprise. "Sure. Yes. Tala, please. Yes, so, the pattern is too precise to be accidental. It looks like someone was testing how much power they could divert without triggering alarms."

Spike had moved to examine the floor near the quantum box, pretending to sniff it. For a moment, she disappeared behind the table. Frankie and Foss followed. Spike's gaze was focused on a small metal grate near the wall with a thick braid of cables flowing out and into the box.

"Power conduit," Spike rasped quietly when Frankie knelt down beside her. "Messed with."

"How do you know that?"

Somehow, Spike transmitted the action of rolling her eyes without even looking at Frankie.

"Well," Scarlett said, looking up from Foss's tablet. "That's the last RSVP. Everyone's agreed to a briefing in a half-hour. You'll meet the rest of the key personnel then."

Gold finally looked up from Parker's tablet. "Jin and I need to analyze these transmission patterns immediately. Whoever did this has sophisticated knowledge of quantum field theory." They hurried out and toward one of the standing desks that had a dozen floating monitors above it. Seemed extravagant considering Dr. Wint could probably see everything she needed to with her fancy glasses.

"Captain, I'll introduce you to everyone else at the briefing," Scarlett said. "Though Prakara seems to have already decided where to focus."

Spike nudged Frankie, eyes flicking toward Tala, now kneeling by the grate that had caught their attention.

"Could I borrow Dr. Foss until then?" Frankie said.

Foss looked up, startled.

Guilty.

"Of course," Scarlett said. "Then she can show you where the meeting room is."

Scarlett started for the door, and then stopped.

"Please be quick," she said. "We have no idea what these—spies?—are up to. Find them." She shivered. "Or so much could go wrong."

FRANKIE WAITED until everyone else was out of the quantum transmitter room and Scarlett had closed the door before turning back to Tala Foss. Everyone could see them through the big window-wall, but then, she could see them, too.

Spike at her side, Frankie knelt beside the environmental engineer at the back wall. Tala was using something on her tablet to scan a fat, braided, black-mesh cord, a massive power conduit that went from the wall to the transmitter. The cord carried a loud buzz. Warning: Don't Touch.

With both the dull gray bulk of the quantum fabricator box and the wide metal legs of the table that held it between them and the window walls, they were hidden from view. Here on the matte black rubber-over-metal floor, partially shielded from the aggressive ventilation overhead, the air was warmer. Almost human-friendly. Not that buzz, though, which traveled up Frankie's knee and rattled through her bones.

"So, these power anomalies," Frankie said. "They start here?"

Tala startled, and blinked up at her. She tucked an unruly blond curl behind her ear and nodded toward her tablet. Then she seemed to realize Frankie couldn't read the tablet, and shook her wrist, which pulled up a small floating data screen between them.

"Here, I can pull up the schematics," she said, too soft. Her voice had a beautiful cadence, if you had the sharp ears to hear it.

Spike plopped a little behind Frankie. The cyvlossic still had a view through the clear walls of the lab. This room wasn't sound-proofed, and Spike's smooth, tufted ears swiveled toward every noise. Gold's sharp interjections, Wint's clipped responses, the soft hum of equipment.

Tala's fingers tapped across the screen like mercury. The smell of fresh soil intensified as she leaned forward, to point at the screen. Her handmade bracelet of recycled metal caught the light but didn't make any sound.

She tapped glowing blue markers along intertwining amber lines, her hand steady but her breaths shallow. "See these junction nodes? When one reads that the power flowing through it is too low, it throws an alert. Then the system siphons from a nearby line to make sure everything is in balance."

Spike rested her chin on Frankie's shoulder, the weight of it almost knocking her out of balance herself.

"That's how it's supposed to work." Tala looked away from the hologram, her eyes wide, at Frankie—or at Spike. "But we've been seeing these odd fluctuations. Losses. Each not quite enough to trigger the alert, but they're at lots of these nodes."

Frankie frowned. "So you're leaking power?"

"Or someone is collecting it. All together, these little draws can add up."

"Enough to power… what?"

Tala shrugged. "Maybe another lab?"

Chief of Staff Scarlett might have something to say about that.

Spike growled softly, pawing at the interface, trying to expand one section. Tala blinked at Spike, but adjusted the layer as requested. One of the sets of cargo bays?

Spike retreated, unbalancing Frankie again. Tala quickly wiped the hologram away, something odd in her expression.

Frankie tried to figure it out. "And you reported this?"

"Yes." Tala bit gently at her lower lip. Something raw and frustrated flickered behind her careful expression. "Three times. Four! To Bulwarion, even to Dr. Wint. Every time, dismissed. 'Environmental systems always show anomalies in a lab this complex,' they said. Like anyone's ever had a lab like this."

Frankie felt a pang of sympathy. Tala was at least twenty years younger than the rest, and probably without the fancy pedigree of Gold or Wint. "Not taken seriously?"

"When am I ever?" She shrugged.

"'All Voices Heard,' right?" The Cooperative Realm's motto.

"Sure," Tala said. "Unless your doctorate is from some backwater system, and you're more interested in keeping everyone on this rock alive rather than 'Pushing the Boundaries of Space and Time.'" The motto of the Interstellar Science Society.

"And now they're worried."

"Now their funding is in danger." Tala slouched, her back against the back wall.

Frankie's knees were killing her. She stood up, stretched, and then tapped the side of the gray quantum box with a finger. Sitting on its knee-high table, it reached her chin.

"Why is this so big?" she asked. "If you're just sending data? Or nanites, whatever."

"Room for growth. There's the makings of one triple this size in the warehouse, just waiting."

"And you really think we can zap giant objects from moon to moon?"

Tala leaned forward a bit and pulled out the scrunchie

holding her shoulder-length curls back. Sweeping her hands along her head, she tried to corral all her hair again.

Behind her, Frankie heard Spike snort.

Humans shed, too.

"Why not?" she said.

Frankie looked out, to the lab full of bundled-up people. Gold and Wint were hunched together but looking at separate screens of quantum field equations. And sniping.

"But you knew it wasn't normal, this fluctuation," Frankie said.

Tala pushed to her feet. The inset wall lights hit the metal of her bracelet as she moved, making it shine like a setting sun.

"I've managed environmental systems on five different research bases." A hint of pride crept into Tala's voice. "You learn to distinguish between random crap and real patterns."

"You're from the outer colonies?" Frankie asked, finally placing the subtle accent in Tala's speech. Roger's Quarter.

Tala nodded. "Maris Settlement. Not exactly a technological hub." She shoved her hands into the pockets of her brown coveralls. "My parents were hydroponic farmers. University was out of reach for them. They were so proud when I earned a scholarship to RQ U. 'Equal Access, Universal Progress,' and all."

Frankie was sure Prakara Gold wouldn't be able to find Roger's Quarter University on a map.

"That's why I notice these things. When you grow up making do with limited resources, you get good at spotting inefficiencies."

She hesitated, then added, "Sometimes I think the bigger problem is that most of the senior researchers have never had to worry about resource allocation. They assume unlimited power, unlimited funding."

"While the rest of us live with limits," Frankie said.

"Exactly," Tala said, voice soft but a spark in her eyes. "When you come from scarcity, you notice every wasteful practice. Every slight inefficiency."

She looked at the quantum box. "Whoever did this has intimate knowledge of our monitoring systems. They knew exactly how much they could take without triggering alarms."

"Inside job," Frankie said.

Tala nodded. "But the technical expertise required to tap into the quantum field? Not a lot of people here could do that."

Good. That would narrow the list of suspects considerably.

Assuming this had anything to do with the sabotage.

Spike drew closer to the grate and that big buzzy cord. She scratched at the floor near where the cord met the grate. The flooring looked more more gray—or more worn—than the rest of the flooring. She made that low rumble-grumble that said, "Look at me."

"What is it?" Frankie asked, moving to join her.

Tala followed, frowning at the flooring. She fished some other compact analyzer from one of her myriad pockets, and ran it over the spot. And froze.

"Ceramic composite residue," Tala breathed, alarm dampening her tone. "High-grade EM transmission shielding—experimental, cutting edge." She frowned at Frankie. "The kind Huxley Parker was bragging about at the last staff meeting."

"Parker? The overdressed one?" Nice beard, nice clothes, extra polish.

Tala nodded. "He's been here maybe two years. Transferred from Central District and brought all kinds of fancy equipment with him." She pocketed her analyzer. "And seems to get more all the time, even though we all have a weight limit on deliveries. Being a deserted base and all."

Tala frowned at something only she could see. "Typical, how quickly Wint welcomed him into her secret clubhouse." She startled, and glanced at Frankie. "Figuratively, of course. We none of us have any secrets here."

Frankie let that go, but thought about the first part. She'd seen the reluctant handshake, Gold's barely hidden disdain. Tala clearly hadn't.

"Meanwhile, I've been raising alarms for weeks, and..." Tala trailed off, shrugging.

Spike made another rumbling sound, her ears flattening slightly. She must have pulled data off Tala's tablet. Frankie recognized that look—Spike had seen something familiar.

The cyvlossic squeezed her eyes shut a moment. Then Frankie's wristcom pinged. A message, from Spike. *Power draw = pirates.*

Pirates. Great.

"Tala, these power taps, their precision, does the pattern remind you of anything?"

"Smart thieves?" She looked honestly bewildered.

"I might've seen something like it before," Frankie said, vamping. "In the outer systems. Edge space pirates use similar techniques to steal power without detection."

Tala's eyes went even wider. "Pirates?" Her voice jumped.

"Maybe not literally pirates, but someone familiar with their techniques."

"Someone familiar with pirate efficiency routines?" Tala's voice was nearing screech registers. "You think it's someone from Outer Systems?"

"Or maybe just someone with outside knowledge," Frankie said. "These junction points—who can access them?"

"Maintenance personnel, mostly. Some senior researchers." Tala paused. "But anyone with basic systems knowledge could find them if they were determined enough." Her vision went fuzzy again. "An efficiency algorithm."

She leaned her back against the quantum transmitter, her face going soft.

Spike's ear's perked in alarm, but Frankie shook her head.

Incoming scientist fugue state.

"The quantum technology we use is incredibly power-hungry. That's why it's limited to research stations with massive energy resources. But what if someone found a way to make it run on less power?"

Spike's ears perked forward.

"Is that possible?" Frankie asked.

"Theoretically," Tala said. "I've actually been working on some calculations in my spare time." She hesitated, glancing around as if checking who might be listening. "The current approach is so wasteful," she said. "We're using brute force methods when we could be more… elegant."

"And that would change what's possible?"

Tala nodded. "Everything. Right now, we can transmit data packets easily. Nanobots with effort. But larger objects? The power requirements are astronomical."

She leaned closer. "But what if they weren't? What if we could send a tool? A weapon? A person?"

"A person?" Frankie's mouth went dry. She swallowed hard.

"That's the theoretical endpoint," Tala said. "But no one believes it's possible. The complexity of maintaining quantum coherence across billions of cells, the computing power needed to reassemble a living being…"

She shook her head. "Wint and the others are fixated on the next milestone—inanimate objects smaller than a marble. But even that's a massive challenge."

"Unless someone's found a way around the power problem," Frankie said. "An efficiency."

Tala's eyes met hers. "Exactly. Then it could even—potentially

—be used outside of secret government-controlled research facilities. Everywhere."

Emergency food, blinking into existence right where it was needed.

Emergency shock troops.

Before Frankie could even start digesting that terrifying scenario, the door hissed open again.

A muscular, powerfully built woman knocked on the window beside the door. Her dark skin contrasted with close-cropped silver-gray hair and a bold ropey scar tracing the left side of her wide jaw. And also with her clear, obviously cybernetic hands.

She nodded once to Tala, who returned the greeting.

"Finn Marsh," Tala whispered to Frankie as the woman walked the length of the window, scanning for something near the floor with some multitool. "Maintenance. She probably knows more about this base than anyone."

Marsh? Frankie quick checked her electronic background files for a Marsh. There. "Marsh, Finn (formerly Kell, Darius)."

"Darius Kell?" Frankie read aloud.

"Shhh," Tala said. "That's her old name, before…" She dropped her voice even more, and leaned toward Frankie's ear. "She served time for tech theft and black market dealing." She seemed to realize how that sounded, and quickly added, "But Scarlett trusts her completely. Gave her a second chance when nobody else would."

Marsh didn't seem to have found what she wanted. She took two steps into the room, still scanning downward. And stopped.

Spike growled.

"What in all of voidspace is that!" Marsh said.

"Companion animal," Frankie said at the same moment Tala said, "Pet."

Marsh scowled. "It triggered a system anomaly. Get it out of there."

"Sure. We're just leaving," Frankie said before Spike thought of anything rude. She stepped protectively between Marsh and her companion animal, praying the maintenance person would not soon have another scar. Spike pranced out the door.

"Foss!" snapped Jin Wint from her desk halfway down the lab. "Are you quiet finished with your … tour guiding?"

Tala's expression shuttered, a practiced blankness hiding her sun. "Yes, Dr. Wint." She turned apologetically to Frankie.

"Go ahead," Frankie said. "Thanks for your help."

Tala raced off, toward Wint, but then stopped, and raced back.

"Conference Room Delta. Take the main corridor, to the Commons." She pointed to the door at the front wall of the lab. Not the door they'd come in, set into the outer wall. "Past the dining hall, past the first open space, and maybe another space, or the gym? Anyway, when you get to the inner edge on that side, you'll see a row of frosted-glass doors. It's fourth door after the big vine wall."

Great. Another puzzle.

CHAPTER
FOURTEEN

FRANKIE MADE it to Conference Room Delta with two minutes to spare. That vine wall art installation thingie had been mesmerizing. It never stopped moving, but wasn't really moving at all. Spike had had to practically drag Frankie away from the thing.

The air shifted abruptly as she stepped into the room. Frankie's nose crinkled involuntarily as the standard closed-meeting-room scent of over-recycled air gave way to an assault of fake lemon topped with the warm plastic sheen of equipment running just a touch too hot.

Unlike the standard stark utility of the lab and corridors, this room seemed designed to impress visitors. Weird, since visitors weren't really welcome at a secret base. The smooth, yellow-cream walls seemed to glow under lights set along the edges of the ceiling. The padding on the sixteen sleek, rolling, adjustable chairs matched the walls. The long, dark oval table that took up most of the space gleamed with an inlaid star map that pulsed with soft blue light, tracking real-time positions of local celestial bodies.

"Nice," Frankie said, dropping into the chair at the foot of the table, closest to the door. She slid her hands appreciatively along the soft padded armrests.

Environmental specialist Tala Foss snickered as she seated herself at Frankie's left, blond curls bouncing. "Official name for this room is 'The Golden Catalyst.' Check out the plaque behind you." A copper-colored square was riveted to the wall next to the door, with stamped black lettering large enough for Frankie to read clearly even a meter away. "A gift from Prakara Gold: Because genius needs a proper stage."

The emerald silk-clad diva was already seated, at the head of the table. She'd unpinned her thick black braid—stress?—and it now draped over her crossed arms. Gold was very obviously not looking at Jin Wint, seated in the next chair to her left.

It was hard to say what Wint was looking at, behind her green-rimmed AR glasses, but she was scowling. The tension between them vibrated in the air like a plucked string. Wint had not loosened that tight knot of hair at her nape; Frankie got an echo of a headache just looking at it. Was withstanding painful hair some kind of pissing contest for geniuses? If so Gold had lost this round.

On Wint's opposite side, Huxley Parker seemed oblivious to the overtones. He leaned forward at an angle Frankie inwardly dubbed deliberately handsome. His pricey burgundy jacket sleeves pushed up just so, his data-neural implants, soft against his temples, somehow glimmering in a complementary color. He must have reupped his cologne on the way over. His metallic cedar scent fought with the room's aggressive, now annoying, lemon for dominance.

Gold ignored him, too. Instead her gaze was fixed on something behind Frankie.

Or someone.

Scarlett Bulwarion stepped into the room, moving like a

graceful freight train. The chief of staff. Her perfectly cut black labcoat billowed slightly behind her confident stride, her well-behaved henna-red hair glowing in the warm lighting.

As she neared the head of the table, and without breaking stride, Scarlett grabbed the empty chair to Gold's right and dragged it with her to the head of the table. With polite ruthlessness, she nudged Gold's chair sideways, towards Wint. Both Wint and Parker had to scramble to avoid collision. Chairs bumped sharply, voices huffing in indignation.

Nobody said sorry.

"Right," Scarlett said. "We're almost all here."

Next arrived a lean, tall person, with pale skin and paler hair, wearing AR contact lenses. Beige labcoat in the same cut as Scarlett's, black cargo pants underneath They moved with disturbing efficiency around the room, distributing data sticks without a wasted motion. The scientists plugged them into their tablets.

"Lee Calavera," they introduced themselves to Frankie, voice precisely modulated. Pretty mouth. "Chief Bulwarion's assistant." Her enforcer, obviously. "Your security credentials are loaded onto this."

They handed Frankie an oversized, outdated tablet that hummed with subtle energy against her palm. "Your companion is registered as well," they said.

"Thanks," Frankie said. Calavera's gaze lingered a moment too long on Spike. "Quick question—has anyone else arrived recently? Besides us?"

Their eyes flickered briefly. Frankie thought she could see bits of colorful data crossing their irises, but that was surely imagination.

"No visitors in the past twenty-two days." They lowered their voice to a whisper that raised the hairs on Frankie's neck. "Not officially, at least."

Before Frankie could ask what that meant, the air pressure in the room seemed to shift.

Finn Marsh had arrived.

She slipped in silently—too silently for someone of her size. Spike tensed beneath the table, claws extending slightly into the plush flooring. The woman had changed since their encounter at the lab. Now she wore a perfectly pressed navy maintenance uniform, with matching fingerless gloves despite the room's comfortable temperature. The scar along her jaw looked angrier under the room's sunny lighting.

Marsh took a position against the wall behind Tala rather than sitting at the table, her eyes constantly moving from face to face with predatory awareness. Her posture reminded Frankie of spacers who'd spent too much time in dangerous ports—always ready, never relaxed. The woman's gaze met Frankie's for a split second, then deliberately shifted away.

"Great," Scarlett said again. "Let's get started. Finn, would you close—?"

"Actually," Frankie said quickly, "could we leave the door open?" To help ease the tension, and also give Spike a chance to slink off and see whose workstations were not locked down.

Scarlett waved agreement, refocusing swiftly. "Here's the issue: five days ago, our experimental quantum transmission— the one no one but us should know about—was intercepted. Our data packet was replaced en route. The false data was injected seamlessly under authentic encryption."

"Corrupted data," Dr. Wint corrected, her clipped accent making the words sound like an accusation. She adjusted her AR glasses with a precise motion. "The package contained nonsensical readings, designed to appear legitimate at first glance."

Gold leaned forward in a rustle of silk and singing of bracelets. "Which suggests deep internal familiarity with our protocols."

Frankie nodded. Familiar territory. "So the saboteur had precise knowledge and internal base access."

"Clearly," Wint said, short. A brief silence as people spun out the implications. Exchanging suspicious glances.

Scarlett continued, calm as if she already knew the answer. "But why intercept? Why not just send a rogue packet on its own, without all this fuss?"

Frankie nodded. "Yeah. If somebody wanted to sabotage you, why not just broadcast whatever false data they had anytime? What's stopping them?"

"Each quantum transmission channel requires a specialized authentication," Wint explained. "Mine. It starts with a unique quantum key generated internally by the sensor array."

"So," Frankie tried to follow, "no outsider can just start sending rogue data? They'd have to trick the system to insert their packet inside an authorized transmission. Authorized by you."

"Just so," Wint said.

Tricky. And something that communications specialist Parker might know a lot about.

Gold cleared her throat. "There's something else you should understand about our progress. We've established three phases in our development timeline."

She swung her braid over her shoulder, freeing her hands and nearly taking out Wint. Gold raised one finger. "Phase One: data transmission. Completed and verified. Near-perfect success rate."

A second finger, with a pair of silver rings around it. "Phase Two: nanobot transmission. Recently achieved. We've sent complex sub-submicroscopic machines between boxes. They maintain all functionality."

A third finger. "Phase Three: macroscopic object transmission. Theoretical but..." She exchanged glances with Wint.

Wint adjusted her glasses. "We've run simulations suggesting it's possible. The quantum field could potentially envelope objects even up to the size of a small drone."

"And beyond that?" Frankie asked.

"Beyond that lies Phase Four," Gold said quietly. "Organic matter."

A longer silence followed.

"But that's years away," Scarlett interjected. "If ever."

"The point is," Wint said, "whoever stole our data now knows exactly how far we've come. And what might be possible next."

"So" Scarlett took the floor again. "The criminal or criminals can't create the startup key remotely."

"Yet," Gold said.

Scarlett pushed on "To get their forged data past security layers, they have to intercept the authorized transmission during that brief initial window, then replace or piggyback their false payload underneath the authorized handshake as if it was never tampered with."

Wint shook her head slowly, disapproval and frustration mingling in her voice. "Intercept or insert—sabotage either way, but technically far more challenging than a simple broadcast."

Inside job.

Frankie leaned forward, the chair adjusting smoothly beneath her. "Could someone be developing their own quantum transmission technology?"

Gold scoffed, the sound echoing sharply in the room. "Impossible. The resources required—"

"Not necessarily," Tala said quietly.

Everyone turned to look at her, and she seemed momentarily startled by the attention, shrinking slightly in her chair. The recycled air seemed to still around them.

"I mean," she stammered, "theoretically, if someone found a way to reduce the power requirements…"

"Fantasy," Gold dismissed with a flick of her fingers, as if brushing away an insect. "Science fiction."

"Actually," Marsh said, her gravel-edged voice rumbling through the room, "We've seen some very specific irregularities in the secondary power and cooling junctions. Steady, systematic drains hidden beneath alarm thresholds."

Frankie caught the quick glance between Marsh and Tala.

"As I was trying to explain earlier," Tala said, with just a hint of frustration coloring her voice.

Gold waved a hand dismissively, gold bracelets singing in the light. "That's hardly—"

"Show us," Scarlett interrupted, nodding to Tala.

Tala swiftly expanded a softly glowing hologram over the center of the table. A blue-line schematic of the base, with orange, gray, and white lines showing the various power conduits.

The same display she'd shown Frankie and Spike earlier. Frankie looked down at Spike for confirmation.

The cyvlossic was gone.

"This is our power distribution network," Tala said. "The quantum lab draws from here," she highlighted a section, "but we've been seeing small diversions here, here, and here." Three other sections lit up in sequence, pulsing red.

"Those are all cooling system junctions, too," Marsh said. She looked like she was about to draw closer, maybe to touch those red dots, but thought better of it. She leaned a shoulder back against the wall.

"Exactly," Tala said, her voice growing more confident. "Someone's been drawing small amounts of power from multiple cooling junctions—each pull too small to trigger alarms."

"But together?" Frankie asked, watching Marsh from the corner of her eye. The maintenance worker had gone very still, her scarred face unreadable.

"Together, enough to power a small-scale quantum field generator," Tala said. "Maybe."

Gold and Wint exchanged looks—a silent communication that spoke volumes. "There would be traces in the base's quantum signatures," Gold said.

"That's… concerning," Wint admitted reluctantly. Her eyes went blank a moment, searching for something her implants could tell her.

"Who has physical access to these junction points?" Frankie asked, her gaze flicking between Marsh, Lee Calavera, and Huxley Parker. Comms lines followed the same rules as power lines.

"That's the thing," Marsh said, the subtle whir of her hands turning palms up punctuating her words. "Everyone with maintenance clearance. Which is about thirty people."

But only one was a convicted felon.

From her position against the wall, Finn Marsh shifted slightly, her weight moving to the balls of her feet.

The tension in the room thickened like cooling gel.

"We need to review all security logs," Gold declared. Her voice carried the expectation of immediate compliance. "We need a full review of all system logs starting at least a month back. Wint, you and I will analyze the quantum signatures to spot any foreign patterns." She glanced over to Scarlett, as if realizing she'd stepped on toes. "Agree?" she said.

"Already started," Wint said with a hint of self-satisfaction. "Parker's running a correlation analysis on communications during the power fluctuations."

Huxley Parker nodded eagerly, neural implants pulsing brighter. "I've found some unusual encrypted packets. Nothing that breaks protocol, but the timing is suspicious."

His gaze flicked briefly toward Tala as he said this, a calculation in his eyes that didn't match his eager-to-please demeanor.

"I'm on physical checks," Marsh said. Each word measured and precise, the slight accent of the outer colonies barely detectable. "Get eyes on the junction boxes, what leads in and out."

Frankie didn't miss the flash of distrust that crossed Parker's face, or the way Wint frowned. But Scarlett nodded, her authority unquestioned.

"Good. Full sweep," Scarlett said. "Captain Styles—Frankie—you are welcome to join any of the investigation teams."

Frankie pinged Spike: *Time's up.*

Everyone seemed to move toward Frankie and the exits a little faster than necessary. Frankie sat still to let them all pass. Only Tala remained seated, taking her time gathering her tablet and then the three empty water bulbs other people had left scattered along the table. She frowned at the bulbs as she dropped them into the recycler. The slight sound, unnaturally loud in the emptying room, seemed to startle her. She caught herself, gave a small smile to Frankie, and hurried away.

As Frankie stepped out, into the corridor that opened out into a "casual recreation module," the temperature dropped noticeably. The station's environmental systems seemed to be struggling, patches of cold air alternating with warmer currents. Or perhaps it was deliberate—keeping people moving, preventing them from lingering in hallways.

Lee Calavera lingered in the hall outside the door, their AR lenses flashing rapidly as they watched everyone leave. The assistant's distracted gaze kept returning to Marsh, who had stopped a few steps down the corridor to stare at some schematic on their industrial-grade, waterproof tablet.

"Captain," they said quietly as Frankie approached. "You seem to have lost your companion."

Frankie caught a blur of sleek striped fur heading their way. "Behind you," she said.

They turned to see Spike, butted up to the wall directly behind them, casually licking a front paw. "Ah."

Calavera leaned—or loomed—over Frankie. "A word of caution."

Great. "About?"

"Security protocols have been… inconsistent lately." Their voice dropped further. "Access logs showing people in two places at once. Missing time stamps."

"Has that happened before?"

"Never." Their lenses flickered.

That they knew of. Who would ever check the time logs? This was a research facility, not a prison.

"The irregularities began exactly twenty-two days ago," Calavera said, glancing at Marsh.

The same timeframe as the power fluctuations. Frankie nodded her thanks, watching as Calavera slipped away to follow Scarlett.

Spike's tail twitched, a signal easy to follow. The pieces of this story didn't add up.

Frankie agreed. She couldn't follow the math, but she could follow the people.

"Let's tag along with Marsh," Frankie said. "I want to see these junction boxes for myself."

CHAPTER
FIFTEEN

FRANKIE AND SPIKE followed Finn Marsh, grumbling to herself, away from the lemon-plush of Conference Room Delta and back into the bustling reality of White Moon Landing's central Commons. The corridor gently curved like a long coastal arc, softly radiant with hidden lighting. Even the floors were that buttery cream color, some kind of tiling that screamed "we never lose gravity here."

Good luck with that.

Through wide openings, Frankie could see cheerful looking people lounging on comfortable looking furniture. The meeting rooms were on the other side of the dining room, the next spot on her proposed itinerary. For now, she pulled a mint protein bar out of her little happy sunshine backpack. Warm, a little smooshed, delicious.

Ahead, Marsh moved with unsettling precision for a person her size, her footsteps nearly soundless on the porcelain-smooth flooring. Frankie hung back just far enough to avoid being noticed. She hoped.

She folded the wrapper over half the protein bar and tucked it back in the pack, banging her hand on the sharp-edged new boxes of honey gummies from Smithson Station.

"Who do you think we're supposed to give these gummies to?" she whispered to Spike. The cyvlossic only flicked an ear in disinterest before trotting ahead to investigate the upcoming intersection, where sleek Commons elegance intersected something decidedly less glossy.

When Frankie turned that corner, the change was immediate, visceral. Like stepping behind a theater's painted backdrop into the bare backstage reality. Here, the soft cream curves gave way abruptly to narrow walls paneled in bare synth-metal composite, rapidly losing sheen to scuffs and scrapes. Round lights on the walls, too bright, threw harsh shadows across bundles of exposed conduits, piping, and ventilation ducts strung along the low ceiling. Instant claustrophobia.

The temperature swung unpredictably, one moment warm enough to summon prickly sweat behind Frankie's ears, the next chill enough to make her want to hug herself. Each breath tasted of machine oil, conductive lubricant, and the faint ozone from active electrical relays.

Underfoot, grated polymer-metal flooring rattled slightly with every step, far too loud for such a cramped space. Each footfall rang against the utility shafts tucked beneath, a constant, hollow percussion. Gray breaker boxes were stuck low to the walls at regular intervals.

Marsh moved with practiced efficiency. Her muscular frame cast a wide shadow against the walls. The distinctive white patch in her close-cropped hair seemed to blink in the erratic light.

Not ten seconds later, Marsh stopped ahead of them. She turned back, and scowled. Spike moved closer to Frankie and scowled right back.

"Guess you're with me, then. Watch your step." Her head was tilted, her shoulders hunched; no space to stand straight.

"How do you even work in here?" Frankie asked, stepping faster to catch up to her. "You can't ever stand up straight."

Marsh shrugged. "Know where all the breaks are. Get my stretches in then."

They walked for a while in silence.

"It's quite the difference, being on this side of the wall," Frankie said. "Kinda gloomy. Have you thought of painting?"

Marsh grunted a maybe-laugh. "You think the beige-on-beige out there is any better?" She smelled like orange drink.

"Ha! Got me there."

Marsh started waving her tablet at each gray breaker box as they passed. it. "I said I could paint a couple walls. Accent wall, you know?" She slowed to wave her tablet at a box, then moved on. "You would not believe the uproar. The meetings! Two short walls, two mild colors, all it was. I had to paint them over."

"Scientists," Frankie said.

"You said it."

She smelled like gummy candies.

Hmmmm.

"I'm thinking of doing up my ship," Frankie said. "My Spear's gray-on-gray, with an accent of emergency orange." Busy picturing her bedroom in a light blue, Frankie almost ran into Marsh.

The engineer had waved her tablet at the nearest gray breaker box, and stopped. She tugged at its front panel. With a reluctant groan, the panel banged open.

Inside, a chaotic tangles of fiber bundles and rapidly blinking indicator lights swarmed like worms.

That couldn't be right.

Marsh cursed colorfully, pressed something on the palm of their cybernetic right hand, and then jammed it with precise delicacy into the mess.

Wonder what happened to her hands? Frankie wasn't about to ask. Yet.

"Somebody's really been mucking about in here." Marsh growled, voice rumbling off the walls in the tight hallway. "Stops now." Something in her hand clicked, and the blinking went down by half.

Frankie looked for the ever-present, tiny dome-shaped security cameras. "Surveillance cams?"

"First thing sabotaged." said Marsh. "Why we came here first." She slammed the side of the box. The hall's acoustics amplified it to a roar. Spike's ears flattened.

"It's not just one, is it?" Frankie said.

"A dozen, maybe," Marsh spat out. "A lot of broken cameras lately."

She slammed the box again.

"Burned solder and synthetic coffee," She rumbled. "They must've been at this for hours."

"And nobody saw them?"

"Nobody said anything." Marsh stepped back from the box, maybe so she wouldn't slam it again. "Got it stopped, for now. Gotta keep on." She shook her head. "Maybe a dozen. Right in front of my eyes."

They started to head farther down the corridor, fast, Marsh in the lead.

"White-based colors can cover gray in one coat," Marsh said, and stopped. She looked behind Frankie. "Where's that monster of yours?"

Spike hadn't moved. The cyvlossic stared hard down into the metal grate in the center of the corridor floor near the bad junction box. She was sniffing all around it.

She suddenly stiffened. Her tail, usually swinging horizontal, slammed to the floor.

Frankie ran back to the cyvlossic. Marsh followed, slowed by having to hunch her shoulders to protect her head.

Frankie crouched and peered through the grate's metal cross-slats. Too dark to see anything.

"What could she be seeing?" she asked Marsh.

"Hell if I know." Marsh grabbed the long metal leveraging tool off her belt and popped open the grate.

They all looked down.

In about a meter-high space, tucked amid the water reclamation pipes, oxygen reuptake tubes, and who knew what else, lay something that looked like a radio with the casing taken off.

Or a bomb.

"Signal booster." Marsh swore under her breath. "Bet it's tapped into the station's internal communications network."

Marsh scooted to the edge of the open grate. She slid slowly into the space, careful to place her feet on floor and not pipes or cables. She sat on her heels and stared for a long moment at the thing. She put her hands over it, as if scanning it.

Then she pulled out a pair of wire cutters, clipped twice, and lifted the thing up and out of its nest. She handed it up to Frankie.

Who didn't take it right away. "What is it?"

"Dormant, now." Marsh pulled herself out of the space and sat, feet dangling into the space. Frankie gave her the object back as soon as she was settled.

Marsh turned the object. In addition to all the wires and three battery tubes, it had a control panel. Blank.

"Thing looks home-made," Frankie said, sidling away a little.

"Nah, just has the cover off. Probably trying to hide the maker codes. So we can't figure out where it came from.

"You recognize it," Frankie observed. It wasn't a question.

Marsh's eyes met hers, calculating. "Similar design to devices used in the outer colonies. For bypassing Cooperative communications restrictions."

"The same kind of tech that got you convicted?" Frankie asked.

Spike snorted. So much for tact.

But Marsh didn't flinch. "Same idea. Better than I could do." She tapped on the screen. No joy. "Whoever built this knows their shit."

Spike made a soft sound, drawing Frankie's attention. The cyvlossic was staring at something on the floor—a small metal clip that might have fallen from the device.

"May I?" Frankie asked, reaching for the device in Marsh's hands. With her other hand she swept up the clip.

After a moment's hesitation, Marsh handed it over. The device was surprisingly heavy for its size, with a metallic housing that felt warm to the touch. Frankie attached the clip to the display panel. The panel lit up.

"Piece fell off," she explained.

"Piece of shit," Marsh growled.

Frankie showed the display to Marsh. Who gasped.

"This isn't just reading communications," she said. She rubbed the back of her neck, squeezing hard. "It's transmitting something."

"Transmitting what?"

"Incredible," Marsh hadn't heard her.

"Transmitting to whom?" Frankie asked, louder.

Marsh looked up at her, a flash of fear in her eyes.

"Anybody."

CHAPTER
SIXTEEN

FINN MARSH, holding the illicit comms device in the crook of her arm like it was a baby, led Frankie and Spike out of the cramped maintenance corridor and back into the open, warm welcome of White Moon Landing's central Commons.

Just stepping into the wider corridor that led to the conference rooms made Frankie breathe easier. Already felt like familiar territory. Here, the the corridors arched gracefully, their composite panels in soothing creams and neutral tans, glowing softly with that tucked-in hidden lighting.

Ship might like that.

That weird almond smell coming from one of the conference rooms, though, maybe not.

Marsh muttered something as they neared Conference Room Delta.

"Sorry?" Frankie said.

"I mean," Marsh muttered a shade louder, "maybe should get a better look at this." She rubbed at part of the ropey scar that ran just under her jawline, and slowed down. She hesitated, eyes wary. "Before handing it over to Scarlett."

"You mean, because it might blow up?" The thing did look like a bomb.

"More like mess with her comms equipment."

Spike sat on Frankie's foot. She looked down at the cyvlossic, who tilted her still-strangely sleek head toward the conference room.

Where there might be unsecured network connections.

Frankie pretended to think, furrowing her brow. "You mean, just send Scarlett a pic and go check it out in your lab—"

"Work area."

Frankie pursed her lips. "Probably a lot safer. Well, except for you."

Marsh eyed the bumpy device. "I can handle it."

No doubt.

Frankie glanced into the conference room. Nobody was in the chairs. The hologram of the base still floated above the long conference table. She pretended to have an idea.

"I'll stop here a moment. Give that map another look, you know. See if I can understand the connections." That sounded reasonable, right? Trying to sound like she wasn't going to run around the base blindly, she added, "We'll go right back to the lab after."

Marsh scowled. "Why do pilots always do that?"

"What?"

"Say 'we.' Like you're royalty or something."

Oops. Frankie touched Spike's shoulder lightly, earning herself an indignant twitch of tufted ears. "Always like to include Spike."

Marsh snorted, half-amused, half-disgusted. "Pilots."

"Oh," Frankie said, as if she'd just thought of something. "You like honey gummies?"

Marsh reared back as if Frankie had bit her.

"What of it?"

Frankie slung her backpack around to the front. She pulled out the six shiny, sharp-edged boxes from Smithson Station, tied neatly into a miniature tower.. "Somebody told me to bring these to the base. I think they're for you."

Marsh paused. Tempted to scan them with her hand? But she merely reached out her free hand and took them from Frankie. And put them in the same close-hug position as the mystery box, on her other side.

Somebody was not going to share.

"Thanks," she said, surprisingly softly.

Then she rushed away, leaving them there, alone.

Spike rocketed into the conference room and under the long table. Frankie almost pressed the panel to slide the door shut, but then thought better of it. Closed doors attracted curiosity, and worse: attention.

Instead, she lingered near the door, rereading the absurd plaque Gold had paid for. *Because genius needs a proper stage.* She frowned, tapping the word stage. Who exactly was Gold performing for, way out here?

From underneath the table, Spike made that weird zzrpt—the sound of a physical connector emerging from one of the cyvlossic's implants. Worse than the paw-finger-things. Frankie refused to look down at whatever cutting-edge card trick Spike was performing down there.

Spike must have found an unencrypted access point to plug into.

Or made one.

Just the tiniest hint of Communications Lead Huxley Parker's rich cedary cologne remained in the room, sadly going down to defeat to the sickly sweet fake lemon deodorizer "scent." Frankie looked around for whatever spigot was spraying that stink into the room. Might accidentally turn the crap off.

Under the table, Spike was starting to rumble. The first couple of times it had happened, Frankie had thought Spike was extra happy. Now she knew it was only the purr of the cyvlossic's processors, percolating in data. Then again, maybe that really was what made Spike happy.

There were two spots on the cream yellow walls that were spitting out that smell, one at shoulder level, the other higher than Frankie could reach. Cleverly hidden access panels were near the floor under both tiny spouts.

Frankie went after the low one first, about halfway down the room on one side. Sitting cross-legged in front of the panel, which turned out to need only a push at one corner to open, she inspected the contraption. Typical bottle-based sprayer, with a tiny battery-based motor and a long clear tube leading up to the spigot. The bottle of "Lemon Summer Dream" held almost two liters of the stuff. Nobody would need to refill this thing for months. Longer now, as Frankie turned the valve to "off."

Very satisfying.

The high spigot was in a far corner, near the end of the table where Chief of Staff Scarlett and Prakara Gold had been sitting. Frankie didn't bother getting up, just lurched her way on hands and knees down the room. The beige carpeting was soft under her hands and the stink was less down here. Still not looking back at whatever was making Spike rumble under there.

She had the access panel open and was reaching for the valve when she heard voices coming down the hall.

Toward them.

Frankie froze, her heart ratcheting up.

No danger yet.

Frankie turned the valve, pressed the panel closed, and swiveled her head to look for Spike, under the table. The wood-like top of the table was held up by four parallel pairs of ugly square metallic legs. Spike was on the floor between the first two pairs, flat on her back, looking like she'd been run over by a steam roller. Front legs over her head, back legs stretched almost as long as her tail, a white cord stretching from her belly somewhere into the floor. Old school direct connection.

Frankie hissed, soft. Spike's ears twitched. She tilted her head and opened her eyes, gazing drowsily at Frankie.

Frankie gestured crazily toward the door, and then put her hand by her ear: Listen.

Spike's ears flicked back. She stopped purring.

Frankie's wristcom buzzed.

Stall them, Spike had texted.

Well, duh.

But as Frankie tried to uncross her legs, one of her feet went pins and needles. Must have fallen asleep. She was quick shaking it out when the voices stopped moving.

Just outside the conference room door.

Now she knew who they were. Scarlett's resonant alto, and Gold's sharper-edged soprano. Tense, each word edged with the careful restraint that comes from an argument you've had too many times before.

"I don't want to fight." Prakara, brittle.

"You always say that." Scarlett, weary. "And then you leave."

Frankie absolutely did not want to hear this. Interpersonal conflict was the worst.

Maybe they would move on.

"Let's just find my stylus," Prakara said.

Shit.

Frankie's frantic gaze located the elegant stylus, under the chair Prakara had been sitting in. She lunched, hopefully silently, to grab it, just as Scarlett's spacer boots stopped in the open doorway. Boots decorated with painted white blossoms and little green vines, Frankie noted with absurd clarity.

She held her breath.

Scarlett was only two long strides away from Spike, who had

curled into herself like she was asleep. The connection cable and its connection in the floor almost hidden by the cyvlossic's bulk. Should've kept her fluffy, and the cord would have been invisible.

For a hot second, Frankie contemplated tossing the stylus out into the hall. Like that wouldn't be noticed.

"Because when it gets too real, you decide for both of us," Scarlett said. "You always did."

"Someone had to!" Gold, in a screech-whisper, was not helping her cause. "You just wanted to edit safety protocols and run another inventory while the window closed!"

Scarlett's foot tapped anxiously in triplet rhythm—emotional metronome ticking. "You caused that accident, Prakara. Twelve people nearly died. And then you left."

Prakara's voice dropped, almost pleading. "I waited for you in Central District. You never came."

Frankie tried to gauge the angle of a toss that would get the stylus just inside the doorway. She wasn't that precise a shot, though. And if Scarlett bent down, she'd see Spike.

Scarlett sighed, brittle. "I didn't have a choice, Kara. Some of us had to answer for the fallout here."

"You think leaving was easy for me? It cost me just as much."

"Really?" A swish of fabric, probably Scarlett crossing her arms. "You got your speaking tour. Your awards. I got hazard pay and internal reviews."

"I said you could've come—"

"Come to watch them hand you medals for brilliant reck-lessness?"

There was a silence so sharp it hurt Frankie's ears.

Scarlett's silhouette leaned on the doorframe. "I trusted you. I would've followed you anywhere—if you'd only let me decide with you. But you made the choice alone. You always do."

"But you would've said no." Prakara's voice went soft. Her smart green heels appeared in the doorway, going almost toe-to-

toe with Scarlett's boots. "And we would've been stuck. You're too careful, Scar."

Scarlett's heel tapped down, and stopped. Her legs pivoted.

They were coming into the room.

They absolutely could not look down.

No choice left, Frankie burst upward—and loudly banged her head on the edge of the table. An explosion of static flashed through her brain.

Brilliant.

She rose awkwardly from the floor, stylus upraised like a flag of surrender.

"Found it!" she announced, hopefully cheerfully, as she kneaded the side of her head. "Your stylus, Dr. Gold."

Scarlett jerked upright, her eyes shimmering, hastily drawing her face into its usual mask of composure. Gold's, startled and exposed, still carried her pain in the tightness of her mouth. But she forced an almost gracious smile for Frankie as she reached out for the stylus.

Frankie scooted down the length of the table. She absolutely did not want to crowd them in the doorway, but she pushed into that zone of emotional pain anyway.

They could not come in.

She handed the stylus to Prakara, who took it. She turned the stylus in her fingers like a tiny baton.

"Excellent. I swear, half my genius is in that stylus." She tucked it away with a practiced snap.

Scarlett's tilted her head, her eyebrows raised at Frankie.

"Yeah," Frankie said. "So, we—I—wanted to make sure I understood the layout of this place." She volleyed the ball back to Scarlett. "Did Marsh show you what we found in the maintenance tunnel?"

"What?" Gold said.

Distraction accomplished.

"She said she would send you pictures, but she wanted to actually take the thing someplace where it wouldn't hurt anybody."

Scarlett pulled her sleek custom-tailored tablet out of a pocket of her black lab coat so wide it must have been especially tailored for it. Her face flashed sudden shock.

"A … bomb?"

"What?" Prakara grabbed for the tablet. Scarlett held her ground, but turned the tablet so both of them could see the image.

Frankie quickly clarified, "More likely a communications interceptor, or an energy sieve."

Gold tapped a finger on her lower lip. "Interceptor. Did it break the encryption? I need to get back to the lab."

She scurried off, not waiting to see if Scarlett followed.

Scarlett sighed as she pushed herself off the doorframe. "Thank you," she said, nodding to Frankie. "Turn the holo off when you leave, please." Then she, too, headed back toward the lab, after Kara, slowly. Almost hesitantly.

Frankie watched to make sure Scarlett kept moving. When the auburn hair started to disappear around the bend in the hall, Frankie slammed the panel, and the door slid closed.

She slumped gratefully into the chair at the end of the table and took a deep, cleansing breath.

Already less lemon.

"Clear," she said. She put her cool palm on her overheated forehead.

Spike's purring got louder again.

And then it stopped.

CHAPTER
SEVENTEEN

WITH THE DOOR to Conference Room Delta now safely closed and her breathing back to normal, Frankie chanced a glance at Spike. She bent down in the chair, peering under the big oval table.

In the shadows, the cyvlossic still lolled on the soft carpet, but the white cable that had connected her directly into the network node in the table's wide metallic leg was retracting with a hissing series of clicks back into Spike's belly. Frankie grimaced and squeezed her eyes shut, refusing to reopen them until the creepy weird noises stopped.

"Finished?" Frankie asked, finally opening one eye cautiously.

Spike's ears twitched forward, then back. She rolled to her feet with casual grace and leapt soundlessly onto the glowing table-top. She shook out one back paw nonchalantly before padding across the surface to the still active holographic projection. Even though she knew they were alone, with the space of seconds to get Spike off the table if someone came in, Frankie felt unsettlingly exposed.

But her curiosity was stronger.

Spike's paws—her stubby bean extensions very precise—glided easily over the display's control pad. Frankie watched, fascinated, as Spike zoomed outward, shrinking the labs, the social areas, the dorms. Now she displayed the entirety of White Moon Landing, top-down, a flower-shaped array of interconnected circles.

With another careful flick, Spike highlighted glowing traces of electrical and data conduits running through the base like the branches of rapidly-growing bioluminescent coral. Most lines glowed benignly green: familiar infrastructure, thoroughly mapped. But suddenly orange lines branched furtively outward, snaking off main junctions, weaving through hidden crawl ways and corridors. Lines converged, intertwining at at distant outer circle.

"What is that?" Frankie asked, pointing to the convergence point.

"Storage bay," Spike rasped. "Rarely used."

She just bet. Frankie studied the location—tucked away in a section of the base that appeared to be little-used, one of the older, outer domes.

An older dome near the edge of the base, separated from busier, well-trafficked spaces with redundant bulkhead that could seal it off. Not exactly prime real estate.

Conveniently ignored.

And now power was able to flow to it.

Potentially a lot of power.

"Looks like somebody built a secret clubhouse," she said. "A lab?"

Spike flicked the trackpad again. The hologram morphed into a standard flat screen showing two long lists, side by side. One marked "Official," the other "Actual." Frankie recognized wristcom tracking data immediately, though some lines looked off. Wristcom data could be spoofed, but most everybody forgot they were even wearing something that could track their location, and so didn't bother.

Most personnel movements matched exactly, but Spike quickly zoomed in on a pronounced, repeated discrepancy. All tied to one name.

Huxley Parker.

Slick, expensive Parker, with his neatly trimmed beard and cedar-forest scent. The comms specialist had officially logged consistent lab hours. Yet Parker—or someone spoofing his credentials—have visited this isolated storage bay seven times in the past week. Seven journeys nobody had seemed to notice.

But why?

Spike flicked once more, back to hologram view. She conjured a delicate spiderweb of thin, vibrating data lines—communications threads—overlaying the base's ghostly outline. Most channels looked normal: base statistics and readings, Central District reports, routine internal messages murmuring steadily like electronic heartbeats. But one faint data stream stood apart, pulsing irregularly in ghostly bursts of amber light, radiating unmistakably from the supposedly empty storage bay, curving through the quantum lab—and then disappearing off the map altogether.

"Wait. Where is that signal ending up?" Frankie wasn't sure she wanted to know the answer.

"Off-world. Out-system. Deep encrypt."

Frankie was up and pacing before she realized she was doing it. "That device Marsh found—it's part of this system?"

"Signal boost," Spike confirmed.

Frankie paced around the table, the pieces starting to connect in her mind. "So someone set up an unofficial comms system. Harnessing stolen power, invisible to regular encryption audits. Sending data." She rubbed the side of her head. "To someone."

Spike sat back on her haunches, tail wrapping neatly around her paws, calmly watching Frankie walk in faster circles.

"And they're sending… what?" Frankie said. "To whom?"

Spike's amber eyes caught Frankie. "Quantum dot sensor data. To Skolls."

Frankie's boots froze mid-step on the carpet. Her whole body went cold.

"The Skolls." The shipping conglomerate that had nearly killed them both; that had a stranglehold on edge space commerce; that never took their eye off the ball. "You're sure?"

Spike's tiny shrug radiated both feline disdain and cybernetic certainty. "Pattern matches." She licked a front paw as if she was unconcerned. But her claws were out.

The Skolls could bypass cargo lanes completely if they had a functional quantum transmitter. An army of them. The Cooperative Realm's precarious economic balances would collapse entirely, tilted toward ruthless edge-sector goals.

The balance could shift permanently, beyond any kind of governmental control.

Skoll-world.

Terrifying.

Frankie slouched against the table, apocalyptic images bursting through her mind. She shook her head, hard.

Spike padded over to her. Bumped her head against Frankie's shoulder.

Frankie reached around the cyvlossic. Gave her a quick hug. Took a deep breath.

"We need to see that storage bay," she said.

"And chat with Huxley Parker."

IN THE TIME it took them to get back to the quantum lab, Frankie's mind had settled. But her gut was still roiling.

Spike had silently peeled off earlier, into a corridor that would take her to the weirdly power-hungry cargo bay. A companion animal with no wristcom, she could play "I'm a lost kitty" if anyone saw her.

As the door to the lab slid open, Frankie drew a steadying breath. She stepped through, and stopped. The door did not, sliding shut and then doing some hiss thing that probably meant it was sealing her in.

The lab was semi-dark now, lonely. Even colder. Must be what the base had decided was night-time. Frankie's stomach growled.

Frankie found Parker at one of the only lit workstations, one on the edge of the active zone. His role as communications lead obviously considered not central to the mission. He must love that.

Parker had set his standard white plasticrete desk at standing level, but was slouching in front of it. His coppery hair had flattened; must be using that 12HourTough gel. Shoulders hunched resentfully. Wint and Gold must have shooed him away again. Not wanted, but wanting. Not able to make himself leave.

Or not wanting them to discover his secret.

His beard caught the blue-white light of the screens surrounding him, giving him a faintly ethereal glow. His neural implants a steady amber at his temples. The scent of his expensive cedar cologne—another dose, this late?—hung in the air near him before being washed away by the standard metallic atmosphere of the lab.

Distract Parker. Keep him talking. Give Spike time to investigate the storage bay. Simple.

She approached with deliberate footsteps, making sure he heard her coming. Parker turned sharply, visibly startled, expression flashing quickly toward fake charm.

"Captain! You're up late."

Frankie pulled out the half-protein bar from earlier, and another whole one.

"Snack?"

"I'm good."

She tucked the full bar back in her pack, and unwrapped the half. Parker pulled out a drawer, and pulled out a bulb of water.

"Thanks," she said. She leaned casually against the edge of his workstation, crossing her spacer-booted feet. Parker was wearing soft-looking loafers. A trusting soul.

"Wint and Gold still playing nice?" She took a bite of the bar. Minty goodness exploded on her tongue. She felt like she hadn't eaten in days.

"I wouldn't know." Resentful. Almost bitter. "My job, as I was just recently reminded, is to write up the results for Central District. And stay out of the way."

"Not much of a challenge, for a comms expert like you." She tried the water. Deliciously moist.

Parker jammed his hands onto his narrow hips. "Exactly! Quantum transmission is a communications problem, at heart. Sending data. De-encrypting, receiving. Maybe—I don't know— the local comms expert might know a thing or two about it. Or, you know, not." He glared at his floating screen as if it were Dr. Wint herself.

"Must be tough."

"You don't even know," Parker huffed. "I write up reports that maybe two people read down at Central. They decide if the news is classified, which it almost always is. Even when it's not, they rewrite my words for the formal news release. They break the scansion!"

Parker's voice was rising, an angry whisper. "They destroy the specificity! They make it wrong! Amateurs." He closed his eyes and sighed.

Frankie's eyes darted over to Parker's floating screen. A narrow box on the left with scrolling data that looked like satellite security pings. Wide box at the bottom, not scrolling, with text:

Frankie's last call to the station. The majority of the screen was a schematic. Some kind of transmitter.

Before she could figure it out, Parker quickly wiped the image away; a serene lake surrounded by trees—probably cedars— appeared instead. Parker watched her steadily, considering. Frankie took another bite of the mint bar; let him try to interpret that.

"We did find something interesting, actually," she said after she'd swallowed. "Thought it might interest a comms specialist." She dropped it like bait.

His gaze sharpened immediately, irritation gone in a flash. "Go on."

"A small device. Looks like a signal booster, or a transmitter. Tapped into a power conduit."

Parker sharply inhaled. In his suddenly too-still face, his eye twitched.

So that worked.

"Can I see it?"

"Marsh has it. Testing it now." Frankie took another sip of water. She tilted her head, pretending to think. "But I was wondering—what kind of range could something like that have? Could it reach beyond the station? Transmit off-base?"

Parker stroked his meticulously trimmed beard. At least he could play the part of a deep-thinking scientist. "Depends on the power input and the signal type. Standard quantum-encrypted communications have limited range without relay stations."

"And non-standard?"

His eyes narrowed slightly. The twitch was still there. "Theoretical, at best. The energy requirements would be prohibitive."

"Unless you were siphoning power from multiple junction points," Frankie suggested.

Parker's smile faltered slightly. "Precisely why such a system would be impractical. Too many points of failure, too easy to detect."

"And yet," Frankie said, "someone's doing it."

Parker took a step closer to her. Past the personal-space zone. He loomed. Cedar notes rolled thickly around her, cloying and disorienting in close quarters.

"You're surprisingly well-versed in quantum comms for a cargo captain. Interest, or experience?"

Both, but she wasn't going to tell him that. Frankie lifted the bulb of water again, took a sip. Changed her grip on it. Plenty left to use as a weapon.

"You pick things up," she said lightly. "Edge space shipping, it pays for you to be resourceful."

"Edge space," Parker repeated, his tone shifting slightly. "Must see a lot of Skoll ships out there."

Aha.

Frankie kept her voice light. She hoped. "Skolls control crucial trade lanes. Hard to avoid."

"Efficient strategy," Parker murmured evenly. "Ruthless, but efficient."

"One way to put it."

Parker studied her for a moment, then gestured to his workstation. "I've been running analyses on the encrypted packets that coincided with the power fluctuations. Want to take a look?" At her nod, he stepped back and pivoted, facing his screen again.

Distraction achieved.

Frankie set the bulb of water down and stepped closer to the screen. He swiped up a schematic that did not look like the one he'd had up there before. A complex array of data streams, color-coded and timestamped. Parker pressed play, and the streams started to flow. He pointed to a series of red pulses that appeared at regular intervals.

"Anomalous transmissions," he said, tapping the space where

the red dots appeared. "Piggybacking unnoticed on routine communications. Highly sophisticated. Deep adaptive encryption."

"Hiding in plain sight," Frankie said.

"Precisely." Parker's implants pulsed as he manipulated the display. "What's interesting is the pattern. It's not random—there's a structure to it that suggests a specific purpose."

"Data extraction?"

Parker nodded. "Most likely. But the encryption is unlike anything I've seen before. Multi-layered, adaptive. Breaking it would require—"

A shrill, invasive alarm sliced through the lab, overriding Parker's words. Red hazard lights blossomed urgently across ceiling panels.

Dread crept into Frankie's chest.

Where was Spike?

"What's happening?" Parker demanded sharply. His gaze went fuzzy as he checked messages via his implants. "Pressure drop. Everyone to Central Core."

They ran. Frankie kept up with Parker for about half the length of the long tunnel, and then fell back. Blamed the boots but knew it was her lackadaisical exercise regimen. She wasn't getting any younger.

Out of breath just getting to the outer hall of the central hub, Frankie was relieved to see Scarlett Bulwarion just inside. Her henna-red hair was tousled but her posture was strong and her chief-of-staff voice stronger.

"Breach in Cargo Bay 12-C," she said.

Frankie's stomach plummeted.

12-C. The exact bay Spike was investigating.

"What kind of breach?" Parker asked, his voice remarkably steady for someone who supposedly hung out at that bay a lot.

"Unclear," Scarlett said. "Pressure alarms triggered, but now the automated systems are showing conflicting readings. Marsh is checking it out."

Frankie tried to keep her expression neutral, but panic was building inside her. If Spike was caught—or worse, hurt—

"I'll help," Frankie said quickly. "Fixed a lot of hull breaches."

Scarlett looked like she might object, but then nodded. "We're not expert in that here." She speedwalked Frankie past four corridor doorways, all locked tight, and stopped at the fifth. She pressed the panel to slide the door open. "We'll keep this door unlocked. I'll join you once I've checked on everyone."

Frankie was already into the corridor when she realized Parker was shadowing her. She glanced sharply over her shoulder, questioning.

"Communications sensors might've suffered during decompression," he explained smoothly.

She couldn't argue without raising suspicion. She couldn't argue because she needed all her breath for running.

As they passed through each emergency door, the alarm grew louder, more insistent. In each new segment, the air felt thinner, colder. Pressure drop or panic-induced illusion? Frankie pushed on.

They hit the junction to Torus 12. "Strange place for a breach," Parker commented as the final doors opened. "These storage bays are rarely used."

"Low staffing, low maintenance?"

He didn't respond, just turned into the corridor that ran around the edge of the interior. Cargo bay C was second down on the right. Between the doors, they passed two sets of six lockers with emergency gear and an air station. No sound, just the pounding of their boots.

Marsh was waiting for them, arms crossed. Scarlett arrived not moments later, only slightly out of breath. "Status?" she demanded.

"No breach detected," Marsh reported. "But we can't be sure. The bay's internal sensors are haywire. Pressure readings fluctuating wildly."

"Sensor malfunction?" Scarlett asked.

"Or someone messing with the systems," Marsh countered, her eyes narrowing as she scanned the gathered personnel. Her gaze lingered on Parker for a moment too long.

"We need to check inside," Scarlett decided. "Suit up, Finn."

"I'm coming too," Frankie volunteered instantly, her pulse skating. She needed to get in there. Needed to find Spike. Before it was too late.

Scarlett hesitated.

"It's a big room, right?" Frankie rattled on "More bodies is faster work."

Marsh snorted.

Scarlett pushed her hair back from her forehead. She'd lost her headband, maybe in the run. "She's not wrong. Captain, you accept all risk? Fine. Parker, coordinate with Marsh so we can watch. We'll go back to the first safety door."

Parker's expression flickered with something—frustration? concern?—before he nodded and stepped back. "Of course."

As Frankie hurried toward the closest set of emergency lockers, she caught a glimpse of the bay's exterior through the small observation window in the door. Cargo Bay 12-C gaped, vast and dark, shadows hiding whew knew what inside.

And somewhere in those shadows was Spike.

CHAPTER
EIGHTEEN

ABSOLUTELY NOT WORRYING—FRANKIE repeated it to herself—absolutely not worrying about whatever trouble Spike had managed to find, she fumbled to yank open the wide, gray emergency locker beside the doors to Cargo Bay 12-C. The lockers looked standard—bold yellow, orange, and red reflective stripes —but their crisp clamps and lack of scuffs and patches hinted that it was the bots that did most of the hauling around here.

Frankie's hands shook slightly as she stepped into the bulky suit. This wasn't her familiar, grab-and-go pressure suit like on the Spear. This one enveloped her, sliding plasticky sleeves over her arms. Thick reinforced fabrics hugged themselves to her boots. The whole thing was heavy, like being trapped inside over-sized packing foam that might suffocate instead of protect.

It even smelled like packing foam inside.

Spike was okay, Spike was fine, Spike always knew what she was doing, she repeated to herself. Even if all the screaming alarms and flashing lights suggested otherwise.

She clicked the helmet, half window, half apparently packing foam, into place. The seals hissed, and then the helped beeped happily. Frankie was already too warm, the air was muggy, bitter. A row of anxious text—Breathing irregular—flashed annoyingly across the top of the visor, bright orange letters hovering at eyebrow level. Like she didn't know that already.

"Comms check," Marsh's voice boomed through the suit's speakers pressed close to her ears, way, way, too loud. Frankie winced, and fumbled at the small tablet strapped securely to her wrong forearm, trying to call up the volume controls.

"Loud and clear," Frankie echoed, hoping her panic wasn't evident.

Scarlett's voice clicked in, smooth as polished metal. "Remember, just an inspection. Quick look and out again." Such steadiness. Did Scarlett ever worry about things? Had Scarlett ever had a friend—a fiercely independent, reckless cyvlossic she somehow still trusted with her life—caught in some unknown danger?

Scarlett wisely had retreated to behind the nearest emergency door. She and comms specialist Parker had another air-seal between them and whatever the problem was.

Which was not an emergency. Spike was fine.

"Understood," Marsh replied, though something in her tone suggested she might have her own agenda. "You see us?"

"Both of you," Scarlett said. "Parker's got us helmet camera views. We're right there with you."

No they weren't.

She joined Marsh in front of the looming dark gray double doors to the cargo bay. Marsh keyed in the entry sequence, their cybernetic hands even in bulky vacuum-gloves moving with precision across the control panel. The door's mechanisms groaned to life, hydraulics hissing as the seal broke.

The breeze of pressure stabilizing between the bay and the hall spread a thin mask of sparkling dust across them.

"Pressure already stabilizing," Marsh said. "No breach. Readings normal now."

"How convenient," Scarlett muttered.

"Better take a look, anyway," Marsh said. "Could be some flap or something."

The door clanked fully open with a final pneumatic sigh, revealing the cavernous interior of Cargo Bay 12-C. Emergency lights cast long shadows across stacked crates and equipment. Frankie's suit said the air inside was fine, but no one took their helmets off.

They stepped inside, helmet lights cutting through the gloom. The bay was supposedly an unused storage area, but this one had stuff in it. White-and-gray Skoll shipping containers, big and small. Most were stacked against the inner wall of the bay, quicker for folks to grab and go, but clumps stood at spots along the side walls, too. One big clump ranged right in the middle of the cavernous space. Did the hauler bots get tired and just leave them there?

The hauler bots were usually up against the far wall, close to the opening to the outside. But she couldn't see that far; that wall was shadow on shadow.

Behind them, the door clanked shut with a shiver.

"Take the left," Marsh said.

Frankie nodded stiffly, feeling like an extra in a military show. She shuffled toward the left wall, clumsy in these lead-weight boots. Breath catching, heart hammering at her ribs—"spiking," the visor informed her, ha ha—Frankie tried not to rush. There was air here, and nothing looked burnt or exploded.

But where the hell was Spike?

Where would a cyvlossic hide in here? Low, or high. The ventilation ducts, maybe, or behind one of the bigger crates.

Her wristcom might tell her, but it was tucked inside her suit and the tablet attached to that arm. She would have to call out loud to it, "Hey wristcom, where's Spike?"

Obviously not.

But she so, so wanted to.

She looked for Marsh. Along the far right wall, her long strides had taken her twice as far as Frankie.

As Frankie moved deeper into the bay, passing a collection of crates marked "Office: B style—Misty Morning," her suit's sensors picked up increasing electromagnetic readings. Something in here was drawing significant power.

"You getting these EM readings?" she asked over the comm.

"Aye," Marsh replied. "Stronger up ahead. Stand by."

Suddenly, ceiling-mounted lights flooded on one-by-one in searing washes. Frankie flinched against the brilliant glare refracted from stark white metal walls. For just a moment, everything was magnified into exaggerated, sinister profiles under the harsh light: stacks of crates, distant charging bots, conduits.

Conduits?

Thick cables ran from the side wall to the center of the bay. Frankie squinted to the right. Same line of cables from the right side.

Marsh had already changed course, heading directly for the area behind the shipping containers. If Parker or someone else had built an unauthorized quantum transmitter in here, this is where it would be.

And if Spike had found it…

Heart roaring, Frankie broke into a clumsy jog-shuffle toward the center of the bay. She met a surprised looking Marsh as both neared the containers at the same time. They rounded the container and stopped short.

It stood at the center, softly humming—gray, sleek, restrained menace on a polished gray metal table. Under the table, a matte black box skulked. Cables snaking intricately outwards from the gray box made it look like a malignant creature squatting at the hub of a dense, high-voltage web.

Frankie blinked.

Now it looked like a pint-sized version of the quantum transmitter back in the lab.

Someone had actually made another one.

"What in the bloody…" Marsh breathed.

She moved closer, her gloved hand reaching for the tablet on her wrist. "You seeing this, Scarlett? A quantum field generator. Gotta be. Miniaturized."

"Impossible," Scarlett's voice cut in through the comm. "The power requirements alone—"

"Guess not," Marsh countered. "Someone's done it. Looks like."

"Parker, send this to Wint," Scarlet said off-mic. "And Gold. Let's make sure what we're seeing here."

"Maybe it still needs all the power," Frankie said, sitting on her heels to look for the label on the black box on the table's under-shelf. "This is an Orr box. Baby-sized, but holds all the power you'd need." For the whole base. For a year.

Great. First Skolls, and now Konrad Orr. After Orr Industries had imploded their munitions business by exploding Frankie's home planet "by mistake," it had moved on to developing energy systems. No one had died by Orr box—yet.

Orr boxes were efficient, nearly inexhaustible, and very rare. Only approved for uses outside the Central District, until Orr had twenty years of data proving they were safe. But even in the out-districts, almost no one had them. No one could afford one.

Whoever did this had deep pockets.

Marsh immediately dropped down to look at the box. "Never seen one," she said. "You sure?"

Frankie pointed out the stupid Orr logo—some flying horse, they had a thing for horses—stenciled on a side. Under that were stenciled the specifications for the box, and a dozen different kinds of outlets for worlds' worth of differing power cables.

The box had a smaller footprint than the one in her ship. Tech just got smaller and smaller. Hers had been a gift, from the youngest of Orr's sons, after Frankie had probably saved his life. Before she knew who he really was.

She wondered if this little box also had the requirement that it be professionally inspected every four years. She couldn't afford to fly an Orr tech to her ship, so she'd have to fly into Orr territory. Again. Not looking forward to that.

Marsh tapped the box. "Why siphon power if you've got an Orr box?"

Frankie read the label above the outlets at the back of the box. "Thing isn't a month old. New install. No plugs. Don't think it's connected yet." She stood and tried to wipe her hands on her thighs. "A few days more, and the siphoning would have stopped. Or gone to backup."

Frankie started circling the table, looking for any sign of Spike. Nothing. But as she completed her circuit, she noticed something on the floor near one of the power junctions—a few strands of sleek black and gray fur.

So Spike had definitely been here.

But where was she now?

"Captain," Marsh called to her. She tapped a small screen attached to the front of the device. "Look at this. Does it say what I think it does?"

The console displayed a series of coordinates and timestamps —a log of transmissions. The most recent had occurred less than twenty minutes ago.

During the alarm.

"Someone used the alarm as cover," Frankie said. "To send a transmission without being detected."

"Or the transmission itself triggered the alarm," Marsh suggested, still ogling the Orr box. "This setup can't be stable."

Marsh started to connect her diagnostic tools to the console. "I'll try to trace the destination."

"Wait," Scarlett ordered through the comm. "Don't touch anything else. I'm getting Wint and Gold down to examine it."

Marsh made a sound that might have been a scoff. "By the time they get here, whoever built this could have remote-wiped the logs."

"I said, wait," Scarlett repeated, her voice hard.

Frankie stopped listening. Had Spike been here when whoever sent the message? Did they have the cyvlossic now? Had they thrown her out an airlock?

Nothing on the floor but that stray tuft. Spike wasn't on the floor.

Frankie looked out, way out to the left side wall. Nothing but clumps of stacked boxes here and there.

Spike could be anywhere.

Frankie checked the minitablet attached to the suit's left arm, searching the menu for a scanner option that could sense heat. The app she found could find the hot bodies of the people around her, even through their protective suits. And it seemed to be able to stretch its scan pretty far, maybe even toward the walls.

But nothing else was hot.

Blasted cyvlossic. She better not have gone out the airlock on her own. Prancing outside on the moon wouldn't kill her immediately. But she would need some way to get back inside, pretty fast.

Frankie lifted both hands, running them through her short hair.

Spike was fine. No reason to worry.

The tablet lit up.

Frankie looked up.

Way up.

Ventilation ducts crisscrossed the ceiling. There—a slight movement in the shadows. A flash of amber eyes catching the light. A tiny nod, toward the box.

Relief flooded through Frankie, cool, hot, cold again.

Her visor eased up on the annoying heart rate reminder. Now it was only orange.

But the tiny nod said another thing.

Look closer.

"They're on their way," Scarlett said on the comms.

The clank of the door unlocking finally brought Frankie's heart rate into the normal zone. The heart rate reminder vanished. A few seconds later, after Frankie remembered to breathe, the irregular breathing reminder also vanished.

After Marsh popped her helmet, Frankie did the same. She took a deep gulp of air—and choked on the dust. She always fell for that. In-helmet air was always cleaner, ridiculously so. But the out-of-helmet air was what her nervous system told her it wanted, desperately. Until it had it.

Through the now-open doors, Frankie could see Parker standing just outside, speaking intently with Scarlett. He kept messing with the implants at his temples. His back looked rigid.

"Marsh," Frankie said off-mic, "who has access to this bay?"

"Officially? Maintenance and storage personnel only." Marsh was now circling Orr box, cataloging every detail. "But with the right codes, anyone could get in."

"And who would have the knowledge to build something like this?"

Marsh paused. Her eyes met Frankie's, warily. "Someone with advanced understanding of quantum field theory and communications technology."

"Like a communications specialist with neural implants and too-expensive taste," Frankie suggested.

Marsh nodded slightly, looked away. "Among others."

Her tablet beeped. She looked at the screen. "Thing's been active at least three weeks. Multiple transmissions, all deep encrypted."

"She told you not to do that," Frankie said softly.

Marsh glared at her. "Somebody's lying. Who's to say it's not our local quantum science genius?"

"Can you tell where they were sent?" Frankie asked. She started to circle the quantum box again.

Look closer.

"Not exactly, but…" Marsh's voice trailed off as their diagnostic tool displayed a series of coordinates. "These are edge space transit lanes. Near the Skoll shipping routes."

Right. So the Skolls were definitely involved. But were they working with someone on the base, or had they placed their own operative here?

Her thoughts were interrupted by the arrival of Prakara Gold and Jin Wint, both looking distinctly uncomfortable in their hastily-donned pressure suits, helmets hanging bulky behind their necks. Scarlett wasn't taking any chances with her top scientists.

"By the stars," Gold breathed as she took in the device. "It's beautiful."

Wint pushed past her, already analyzing the setup with her rigged-up glasses. "Elegant design. Reduced power consumption by …. maybe 70 percent compared to our prototypes."

"But how?" Gold demanded, knocking Marsh aside to peer at the screen at the top of the device. "We've been working on efficiency improvements for years."

"Someone solved the field stability problem," Wint said, her voice tight with professional jealousy. "Look at the harmonic resonators—they're completely reconfigured."

Frankie stepped to the side and caught another glimpse of Parker through the doorway again. He was glaring toward the scientists, who he couldn't even see behind the storage crates, with an intensity that made her uneasy.

"Dr. Wint," Frankie called, drawing the scientist's attention.

"Could this device send transmissions outside the base without being detected by your monitoring systems?"

Wint nodded reluctantly. "If calibrated correctly, yes. It's operating on frequencies adjacent to but distinct from our official channels."

"And could it intercept your transmissions? Replace the data packets?"

Wint and Gold exchanged glances. "That would explain the breach," Gold admitted. "This could be the source of the tampering."

Frankie looked up at the ventilation duct again. Spike's eyes gleamed in the darkness, and the cyvlossic made a subtle movement with her head—directing Frankie's attention toward the far side of the device. Away from the control panel.

As the scientists continued arguing over field stability parameters, Frankie found it. Near the bottom edge—a tiny cinnamon-candy-shaped data stick, overlooked. Still plugged in.

Someone had left in a hurry, forgetting to remove their data storage.

Moving casually, she sidled up to the box. Without drawing attention to herself, she pressed the stick fully into the port, then quickly extracted it. She stuck it on the mini-tablet on her forearm, not plugged in.

And she started to walk away.

"We should move the device," Gold said. "Get it to the lab for proper analysis."

"Absolutely not," Scarlett said over the comm.

"Too risky," Marsh agreed. "It's integrated with the power systems. Disconnecting it improperly could cause a station-wide surge."

"Marsh is right," Wint added. "We need to study it in place first."

Scarlett sighed audibly over the comm. "Fine. But I want

continuous monitoring. Cameras, Parker. And I want to know who built this, and why. "

Frankie glanced toward the door again. Parker was gone.

"We should check the logs," Frankie said. "See who accessed this bay recently."

"Already on it," Scarlett replied. "Lee is pulling the security records now."

As the others continued their examinations and exclamations, Frankie made her way casually toward the exit. She needed to find somewhere private to check the data stick—and to reconnect with Spike.

At the door, she met up with a frazzled Scarlett. Must be a shock, finding something so large—so malign—just lounging around inside your base.

Scarlett's vibrations triggered a wave of exhaustion in Frankie. How long had she been awake, anyway? Was she even thinking straight?

Was anyone?

"Sorry to bother, but do you have somewhere I can have a lie-down?" Frankie asked. "I need some time alone. With Spike. You know."

Scarlett acknowledged her with a distracted "Right. We set up a room for you." She frowned, and then her face cleared. She must have some implant, too, with connection to her assistant, at least. "Map's on the tablet Lee gave you. Have a nice night."

Once out of the suit, Frankie took up her tablet. Her room was all the way on the other side of the labs. Odd. Not guest quarters, but with the quantum scientists. Scarlett didn't want her polluting the other research labs? Or announcing her presence, more likely.

Prakara Gold had told Frankie that only the quantum team knew of the breach. Frankie hadn't believed her. Bases didn't work that way. Gossip carried on the recycled air.

But maybe White Moon Landing base was the exception?

Frankie sent the map to Spike's mailbox.

She wasn't halfway there before she heard the slightest whoosh behind her, like fabric swishing.

Spike pulled up beside her thigh.

She was starting to look a little scruffy.

CHAPTER
NINETEEN

THE DOOR to Frankie's temporary quarters hissed open and she stepped inside, blinking. After the excitement—the panic—of the emergency in the storage bay, this room's silence should have been a balm.

But this room wrapped around her like a new sheet—too stiff, too cold, and unfamiliar in all the wrong ways. The door shut behind Spike with a soft thunk, and for a moment all Frankie could hear was the faint hum of the air recirculator and her own ragged breathing.

She blinked, hoping the unsettling sterility was just a first impression.

It wasn't.

She hated it already. No rust stains, old picture hanger hold, chipped panels, cramped cabins smelling faintly of burnt coffee and Spike. This place was as antiseptic as a sealed museum case.

She edged farther inside. Spike padded past her, not bothered at all, on her way to find the network connect. Or the toilet.

The room looked like it had been printed from a template. Four perfect cream walls—no scuffs, no evidence of anyone ever leaning their tired head or muddy boots against them. The lighting was bright, flat, and sterile, with none of the soft golden glow she'd coaxed from Ship's panels back home.

She walked deeper into the apartment, passing through the so-called living area. In the center sat a beige couch—oversized, looked stiff as a board. Custom designed for awkward meetings rather than comfort. Behind it, an aggressively empty desk with three side drawers, surely empty, backed up to the back wall. Its sharp beige corners eager for collisions with careless knees. Just a factory-wrapped gray tablet and a lonely stylus waiting there, perfectly parallel, maddeningly sterile. This place was an entirely blank surface, practically begging her to experience an existential crisis about her lack of timeliness or organizational rigor.

Through an arched opening to the right, a sleeping area yawned into view, equally dreadful in its cream cleanliness and uniform blandness. The square bed at its center seemed to stare loftily back like it had passed judgment and found her wanting. It was wrapped by a sheet so crisply white she immediately wanted to spill something on it just to see what would happen.

She crossed to the plastiglass wardrobe built into the far side. When she clicked the first of the two doors open, a sickly synthetic smell, worse than fresh vinyl upholstery, wafted out, stinging the back of her throat. Inside: four generic jumpsuits, maintenance gray, two pairs of still-stiff slippers, and a robe with the station's logo stitched at the collarbone. Behind the second door, two bright-white pillows and—oh, color!—a beige duvet.

She pulled the bedding out and carried it to the bed. Stacked the pillows against the wall, spread the duvet.

Too clean, too empty. Worse than a hotel room, even. No hint of spilled curry, no trace of ship oil, no comforting lingering fur.

Well, she could fix that.

She shrugged out of her backpack and let it fall onto the bed.

A gift from a little girl a while back, the canvas bag was brilliant yellow, sprinkled with bright-red poppies.

That shocked the room into some life.

She tossed herself onto the bed next to her pack. The mattress couldn't decide whether to give or not. She scootched up against the pillows and rummaged in her bag for the tablet that was not linked to anything else.

Spike jumped up and padded over to her. Frankie set the tablet on the bed in front of Spike. She fished the cinnamon-dot data stick from her pocket, holding it up to the room's harsh light. It looked harmless—just cheap, translucent red duraplast, no label, no marks. But as soon as she popped it on the right spot on her tablet, it started to load.

But not happily. The screen shimmered and spat pixels like boiling water. The tablet threw up a flickering holographic display, rainbow colors bleeding at the edges.

Spike sat upright, eyes wide and intent. Her paw lashed out with improbable speed, bean-fingers popping out, typing an arcane command sequence into the air. She looked for all the world like an oversized cat batting a string, but as if her life depended on it.

The room's ambient light seemed to dip for half a second as Spike's implants interfaced with the tablet. A warning flash, hot red—data wipe in progress— jumped across the image.

Frankie's heart jumped with it.

Killswitch. The dot-data device was self-destructing.

And about to blast the network all around them.

"Spike!" She grabbed at the cyvlossic through the hologram. "Get out of there—"

Spike growled, deep in her throat, the sound vibrating through the mattress. She swiped at the holographic controls, sending a ripple of static through the room.

Suddenly, every light in the apartment—and, by the sound of

it, the corridor outside—went out with a crack-pop. Frankie's tablet went dead. The air recirculators sputtered in protest.

Surge-protected.

In the sudden darkness, Frankie's world narrowed to the green glow of floor emergency strips and the soft hot breath of Spike crowding at her knees. She sank her fingers into the fur at Spike's nape, and pulled her close.

The silence now wasn't clean; it was thick, waiting, charged.

The tablet screen flickered weakly back to life. Spike shot out of Frankie's loose grasp, her bean-fingers moving with predatory accuracy. Data scrolled fragmented beneath Spike's deft manipulations. Code fragments offered tantalizing clues: timestamps, conflicting entries. Parker was there, at the same time he wasn't.

Spike isolated another section: a fragment of code, rough around the edges, annotated in a way that felt familiar. Old black market tricks. Old ghosts.

"Marsh," she whispered. "Or maybe… Tala."

Or what did they know about Scarlett's assistant, Lee Calavera, the one everybody skirted around? She hadn't seen them since the first meeting.

Frankie fell back onto her elbows. Data, sure, but it didn't bring them any closer to a culprit. The person had mad tech skills —which was everyone on this base. They could spoof personal IDs—something even Frankie could do. They did not sign their work.

Frankie stared into the dark, the bland, empty room suddenly sharper, more dangerous. She felt the prickle of adrenaline, the sense that someone else was standing just outside the door—a shadow waiting to slide across this antiseptic sanctuary and claim it for their own purpose.

Spike's low growl was the only warning before the room lights winked back on, as if nothing had happened at all.

THE COMMONS DINING hall at night was a mausoleum with a caffeine habit.

Frankie paused at the wide entryway, scanning the regiment of square and circular beige tables. After a long hour spent restlessly tossing on that ridiculously hard mattress in that ridiculously sterile room, she felt raw, nerves right at the surface and mind racing with suspicion. Her head ached vaguely, and she had no patience.

She'd left Spike behind, fast asleep on the extra pillow.

Or so she'd thought, until a bump at her hip told her otherwise.

The sepia ceramic-tiled floors soaked up much of the low lighting. Not so much romantic as narcotic. The creamy walls tried to warm the space, but the high ceiling soared in a curve of honeycombed glass, letting in a wedge of frosty lunar gloom. Second-moonlight fractured across empty tables, illuminating the dust motes like half-hearted ghosts.

At the far end, connected only by the sleek, gleaming bulkhead of stainless steel and frosted glass of the kitchen block, another world occupied the same space. A gaggle of voices, animated gestures, cheerful splashes of bright sweaters. Happily sleep-deprived scientists from the other pods, plotting how to change their corners of the universe.

This side was seclusion, defined. Scope of mission, not social awkwardness, made these particular scientists sequester themselves: Quantum paranoia. Secrets. Competition. Mistrust. It hung thicker than soy protein paste between every neatly arranged beige duraplast table.

Frankie stepped up to the opening of the cafeteria-style kitchen —someone was actually working at this hour. She took the bowl handed wordlessly from the server behind the dividing pass-through, a steaming green soup that looked irritatingly healthy and smelled like absolutely nothing whatsoever. The staffer waved toward the self-serve shelves farther down the kitchen wall. Frankie picked some blue fruit, some kind of brown bread, hot sauce, and coffee. She poured herself a glass of water. Drinking out of a glass instead of a drink bulb would be a real treat. Just because, she poured herself another glass, of orange drink.

She put water in a bowl for Spike. Nothing else here looked like it would be good for cyvlossics.

Then Frankie looked for seat mates.

They weren't hard to find.

Only three figures were in this side of the dining room, all at one of the round tables for eight. Huxley Parker, hunched over a cup of stale coffee she could smell from here, neural implants winking like a nervous tell. Tala Foss, nursing another steamy bowl of green, her blond curls tucked behind her ears as if that might help her slide her head deeper into her turtleneck. And Lee Calavera, Scarlett's assistant, upright and precise, an empty plate in front of them, staring blankly ahead as streams of invisible data scrolled past their AR lenses.

They looked worn out, grimly silent, individually and collectively unhappy. People used to being overlooked.

They were perfectly spaced, with an empty beige plasticrete chair between each of them. One spot open, an open invitation.

Frankie's boots clacked and echoed as she approached. Ceramic tiles and grav boots weren't the greatest match. The three—clearly not expecting company—stiffened simultaneously, three gazes flicking up, wary as startled prey.

"Hey," Frankie said, sliding into the extruded plasticrete banana chair. mustering her best grin. "Is this the table for highly competent assistants? Should we make a sign?" She shot Lee a wink.

Nothing happened. Lee stare blankly, expression opaque. Parker blinked nervously as he sipped his bitter brew. Tala tried a cautious smile that faltered halfway through.

Frankie winced inwardly. So much for breaking the ice.

Lee set their fork onto their plate with surgical precision. "Quantum lab emergency meeting in fifteen. Don't be late." They stood, smoothing their lab coat—same cut as Scarlett's but in beige—and strode off with the silent efficiency of someone who knew exactly which cameras weren't working.

Spike bumped Frankie's knee. The cyvlossic caught her eye and tilted her head toward the nearby empty chair, non-padded, four-legged plasticrete.

But not for companion animals. Spike sat on all the chairs in the ship—and all the beds, and all the tables—but here she was strictly floor. Well, except for that time in the meeting room, and in the bedroom. And Cargo Bay 12-C.

Whatever.

Frankie set her tray down and picked up the bowl of water.

"Such a good Spikey," she said as she set it between the legs of the chair next to hers.

Spike snorted.

Frankie sat herself, and slipped everything off the tray and onto the fake ceramic tabletop. She set the tray on the seat next to her.

No one said anything.

Great.

Frankie tried the soup-stuff. Yeah, adding sriracha was a good choice. At least it smelled warm.

As soon as Lee was out of sight, Frankie exhaled and drummed her fingers on the table. "Are they always so... charming?"

Tala's cheeks colored. Interesting.

"Lee's... focused," she said quietly. "They keep things moving."

Parker shrugged, swirling the dregs of his coffee. "Not everyone here gets to be first author. Some of us just keep the lights on." His tone was caustic, all unspent ambition and stale pride.

Frankie leaned in, lowering her voice. "Scarlett trust them?"

Tala glanced sideways at Parker before answering. "Scarlett relies on them. Lee's the only one who can keep up. They know everything that happens, everywhere."

"Ruthless," Parker said, grim. "Efficient. First to know everything, last to tell you anything." He scratched the side of his beard. "It's impressive, really. Dangerous, if they ever decide you aren't adding value." He gestured at his empty cup, hand trembling just a little. "Doesn't even need caffeine."

"You don't trust them?" Frankie pressed, watching both their faces. Parker's unsteady defenses were crumbling from fatigue.

"Trust?" Parker laughed bleakly, setting his cup with a click on the ceramic tabletop. "I barely trust myself anymore. But Calavera—they're an enigma wrapped in corporate beige, same as their wardrobe."

Tala hesitated, stirring her soup vigorously. "I... I think Lee cares about keeping Scarlett safe. They've worked together since before the base was even built."

Parker cut in. "Or maybe Lee's just good at covering tracks. Hard to tell if you're watching out for the boss, or watching the boss." He looked up at Frankie, and scratched at one of his neural implants. They always seemed to itch at him. "But you know what I think? We're all just minions here. Some just have better titles."

He said it as a joke, but it landed with the same weight as Frankie's own earlier attempt—heavy, defensive, true.

"Something wrong with your implants?" Frankie said.

Parker immediately stopped scratching, as if caught stealing. He shrugged, failing at nonchalance. "Needs an update. Once I get the money—well, really time off-base."

Where *would* these people go for holiday? Just to get anywhere would take half of their leave. No wonder nobody stayed for more than a few years.

They sat in silence for a moment, the emptiness of the room pressing close. Every noise from the other end dining hall—the laughter, the clatter of plates—seemed like it was happening on another planet.

Frankie swallowed a spoonful of her sriracha-spiked soup, glad for the extra kick.

"Weird, isn't it?" Frankie sighed finally into the heavy quiet, frustration slipping between her own fatigue-clouded barriers. "How the world seems divided by job titles. Like there's a real wall there."

Tala's eyes went wide, green as old limes. "I don't mind," she said, so guileless it was almost funny. "It's quieter here. I can eat my soup and not have to explain what quantum resonance is to people who just want to tell you about their tomato yields or latest bot firmware update. Besides, I never liked crowds."

Parker snorted—then blinked as if startled by the honesty behind Tala's words.

Frankie, watching the other woman, felt something shift. Tala wasn't hiding a secret—she was just honestly awkward, raw in her edges, still surprised to be here at all. She wasn't playing double agent.

But that meant somebody else wasn't what they seemed.

Frankie spooned up her soup, forcing herself to focus on the meal in front of her. Food was fuel. And she was going to need the energy.

"What was that Calavera said about a meeting?" she said. "Aren't we all supposed to be sleeping?"

"Scarlett's on edge," Parker said. "Along with Wint, Gold, all of them. The Central District test is tomorrow, the one that's supposed to get us funding for another three years. And here we are, after all this work—"

"All the practice tests," Tala cut in, sighing.

"And now they're not sure we can pull it off." Parker rubbed at the implant on his temple again, grimacing. "They don't know what's wrong. They didn't know about the other transmitter. They're running scared."

"And so we're up." Tala pushed her hair out of her eyes again. "Until we're not."

Parker snorted. "If Scarlett thought we could figure it out as sleepless zombies, she'd cancel sleep altogether."

CHAPTER
TWENTY

CONFERENCE ROOM DELTA—"PRAKARA Gold's The Golden Catalyst"—looked just as fancy and plush but now smelled much less of lemon and more of anxiety. Frankie stood behind the same chair as before, at the foot of the table and closest to the door. She gripped the buttery-soft yellow-cream back cushion, heart less placid than her posture.

Frankie's invitation to the meeting had been muted by her wristcom, automatically set to bedtime mode and not inclined to bother her.

Good thing she couldn't sleep.

After a long, frustrating day, no one looked good. Scarlett entered like a taut whip, her sleek professionalism and sharp black labcoat worn dull by fatigue and worry. She claimed her spot at the head of the table, not even a glance spared elsewhere —no greetings, no pleasantries.

Prakara Gold, already seated, her long braid starting to fray, glowered at nothing. Everyone else arranged themselves reflexively, repeating the same seating pattern as before. Wint even chose to sit right beside Gold again.

Scientists weren't always as creative as they thought.

Huxley Parker actually slouched in, shoulders drawn in, avoiding all gazes. As he sat down, he scratched at his temple just behind the implant.

Finn Marsh took up her silent sentinel position against the wall behind Tala. Marsh had changed clothes again; now she wore maintenance grays that looked welded, not worn. She rubbed at the ropey scar along her jaw. Her gaze roamed methodically, looking for threats, exits, leverage.

Tala, droopy-eyed, sagged into the seat by Frankie, her chin resting on the palm of her bent arm on the table. Even her curls looked tired. There was something dark green or brown under her nails. She caught Frankie frowning at them and gave her a tired smile.

"Tried to relax in my little garden. Herbs, mostly. Usually works, too. But not today."

Lee Calavera, eyes opaque, expression carefully empty, closed the door and took their seat on at Scarlett's right, across from Gold. They did not scratch at their implant.

Frankie settled into her chair. Spike, more and more her tousled self, slunk under the table and vanished into the shadow of the first set of fat square table legs. Plugging in, again?

"Marsh," Scarlett said. "Why don't you start."

Everyone's attention turned to Marsh. Marsh didn't straighten from her lounge on the wall, didn't even look up. Instead, she tapped on a data tablet. Above the table, the hovering image of the relay-transmitter thing they'd found flickered into life.

Everyone's attention snapped to the display.

"Looks explosive, but isn't," Marsh said. "Specialized intercept and relay tech. It streams data cleanly, leaves barely a digital whisper." Her gaze cut to Scarlett. "Not something standard sweeps would spot."

Calavera muttered agreement. "Basically invites outsiders in. We got thoroughly played."

"And it's neutralized, now?" Scarlett asked, grim.

"Maybe." Marsh shrugged. "We've found another. Looking for more. Anyway, this entry point alone can't do the level of systemic hack we've seen. Someone—likely with admin—you're talking much bigger boots, or old black-market mods that let you match command-clearances."

A nervous rustling up and down the table, rasps of static shifting on synthetic shirts. Wint threw up her hands. Scarlett crossed her arms. Even the so-cool Gold reacted, pursing her lips. Tala looked at Huxley Parker, across the table from her, and her mouth twisted.

Parker was staring at the hologram like it held the code to his life. Beneath his copper beard his face went pale.

Frankie leaned forward deliberately, voice low and even. "I took a look at some of the base data." She swiped up her own screen, big so everyone could read it. "Standard logs, nonstandard outcomes. Someone's set the records to show what they please. People, objects, even incident pings are doubled up. Multiple logins, same ID, same hour. Like the system can't keep its own timeline straight."

She let it sit there a beat, watched the electric pulse of discomfort crackle around the table. "Including, for example, Cargo Bay 12-C this week."

Silence. Marsh glanced at her fingertips. Tala's jaw dropped, quickly recovered. Scarlett slapped her palms silently on the table. Everyone looked, for a heartbeat, like they expected a gun to go off.

"Who could tamper at that level?" Wint asked, voice fraying but sharp. "We'd have detected—"

"Not if they have admin-level tools," Marsh boomed in. "Or top-line hacks."

But Tala couldn't hold back any longer. "Does that mean any of us could be blamed for anything just by being someplace? Even if we weren't even there?" She threaded her fingers through her curls and squeezed the nape of her neck. Her eyes were closed but somehow still looked watery.

"Matches what I've been finding," Lee said. "Infrared pings and log misalignments." They looked at Scarlett. "Most related to that cargo bay."

"Which brings us to Cargo Bay 12-C," Scarlett said. She looked around the table, catching each person in her glare before moving on: Lee Calavera, Tala, Marsh, Frankie, Parker. Then landing and sticking on Wint. "How, pray tell," she started serenely, "could someone have built an entire parallel quantum box? Right under our very noses?" Ending on a screech.

"Well I didn't build it," Wint said, raising her hands in surrender. "It's all I can do to ride herd on the problems with the box we have."

"I want to know which of your assistants has all the required knowledge." Scarlett's palms on the table closed into fists. She turned to glare at at Calavera. "And which have even a hint of disruptive behavior in the past."

"Only the techs?" Marsh asked. Still leaned back against the wall, she crossed her arms.

Scarlett threw both hands in the air, frustration finally cracking through her careful professionalism. "Fine! Everyone—suspect everyone. Comb the base." She put her face in her hands, and groaned. Even her groans were melodic.

Another silence, this one tinged with panic.

Tala broke it first, her voice tentative. "It really is a quantum box? That works?"

Scarlett shrugged. "I assume so."

"I could try to turn it on."

"Absolutely not!" Wint said. "Nobody is going anywhere near that box until after tomorrow's test."

Tala sank deep into her chair.

After a moment, Lee Calavera spoke up. "So, the test tomorrow morning? We postpone it?"

Scarlett, startled, lifted her face out of her hands, her mouth a wide O.

"No!" Wint pounded her fist onto the smooth tabletop, wrathful, eyes blazing behind her fancy glasses. "Central District's reviews show up tomorrow in real-time. We fail now, funding dries up! We stall, and Central thinks we can't do it. Either way, we're finished."

"We can't afford caution," Gold argued more calmly, firmly squeezing Wint's clenched fist. "We'll demonstrate packet stability, say we're nearly ready for the nano-trial."

Wint snatched her hand off the table and held it to her chest as if Gold had hurt it. "We used that excuse last month," she said. "It didn't go over well even then."

Scarlett held her hand to her forehead. "Enough. We proceed."

Relief flashed briefly across every scientist's face; exhaustion etched deeper across the technicians.

"Marsh, triple-lock the those transmitters," Scarlett snapped, seizing control again. "I won't risk whoever is responsible stealing them back."

Marsh lifted an amused eyebrow. "They'd have to put them back together first."

Scarlett ignored the jest. "Parker, install additional cameras immediately. In the cargo bay and along the corridor leading to it. Audio, too."

She stood, meeting over, and glared at Gold. Then turned her glare to Frankie.

"Find the spy. Tonight."

The meeting broke up in a rustle of tension and coded glances.

Frankie waited until most people had gone, the adrenaline in her veins replaced by the cold metallic taste of unresolved anxiety.

Gold also hung back as the crowd shuffled toward the door. As she reached Frankie, she whispered, "Watch that new quantum box, Captain. Don't take your eyes off it." If logs could be altered, what was to say that video and audio couldn't be, as well?

Frankie nodded. "Like a hawk," she said equally softly.

But she was watching the people even closer.

CHAPTER
TWENTY-ONE

FRANKIE SAT cross-legged on the rock-hard floor in the middle of cavernous Cargo Bay 12-C, hunched miserably over the battered portable space heater she'd liberated from between two hauler bots near the far wall. The serving-platter-sized thing looked ancient, covered in dents, rust patches, and sporting a frayed sticker that warned inanely, CAUTION: SURFACE MAY BE HOT. It was freezing cold now, battery completely dead.

She'd set the heater down in front of the table holding the transmission box. Behind her towered the stack of white-and-orange Skoll shipping crates that hid the device from view from the hallway. Hard, industrial scents—metallic chill, dust, vacuum-treated paint—hung in the frigid air.

The entire array of overhead lights were buzzy and bright. Parker would need them to set up his camera array. When he left, it would be just her and her little portable lantern, and the shadows.

No way she was going to be able to sleep in that soulless guest room. May as well keep actual eyes on this blasted box.

If she could get the blasted heater to work.

She'd grabbed her red-poppy sunshine backpack out of that bleak guest room, and was now wearing all her clothes: leggings, cargo pants, two T-shirts, a turtleneck sweater, a long tunic, her puffy jacket, and fingerless gloves. She rubbed her palms together, savoring the comfortable friction and familiar texture. And the hint of curry spices.

Fingertips numb, she unwound the heater's back-up cord. Nothing obviously frayed or damaged—good enough. With a quick plea to the gods of power, she plugged the heater into the Orr box, on the bottom shelf of the square metal table holding the pirate quantum transmission device. The Spike-sized Orr box had four long rows of outlets, ready to take on power-hungry devices from across the star system.

Including the little heater, which jolted to life. It hummed unevenly and started to spew the scent of burnt dust. A tiny miracle. Warmth radiated slowly, caressing her freezing fingers. At least she could solve one puzzle on this base.

Eyes drawn upward, she gazed at the sleek quantum device on the top of the table. How could somebody have secretly built an entire quantum transmitter? One that might be better—more efficient—than the one in Wint's lab?

Why?

Who?

She mentally sifted through her suspects. Not Scarlett—strategically brilliant, yes, but lacking the technical knowledge.

Not Wint, who would have simply replaced her own lab setup with this superior version. If it was superior.

Lee Calavera? Scarlett's assistant had the connections, certainly enough subtlety, and access to falsify records. But quantum mechanics? Unlikely. And what would be their motive?

If it was Huxley Parker, that was easy. Money, fame. But he had the same weakness as Calavera—he lacked the experience of a quantum scientist.

But could he fake it?

Tala Foss was a quantum scientist, a good-enough one to be chosen to work on a bleeding-edge project on a secret moon base. Not much appreciated on the team, sure, but was that enough motive to wreck the project? And what did she know of comms networks? Even if she did know how to modify the logs, didn't seem like she could lie about it and get away with it.

But was she fooling Frankie with that wide-eyed innocence?

Finn Marsh had the access, easily. The maintenance technician could probably fake the skills. But she sure did seem incensed at the power drain—especially because she'd missed it. That slid her down on the suspects list, if she was to be believed.

Gold? Wasn't even here. She said she wanted answers, but didn't seem to be looking too hard. Too busy needling Wint and making Scarlett sad.

So here Frankie sat, in the harsh, bright cold. Waiting for inspiration.

Spike was out prowling the outer walls, looking for clues. Or maybe rodents.

Frankie sighed, pressing closer to the heater. Getting warmer, but not enough to overcome the chill in this massive space.

She needed a smaller footprint.

She stood and looked at the stack of scratched-up cream-and-orange Skoll shipping containers stacked four high. She hauled one off the top. Heavier than expected, she had to let it crash onto the hard floor. The clang reverberated around the cavernous bay. Frankie winced, glancing guiltily around. And then got over herself.

What the hell was in it? She popped the six big latches around the waist of the box. Non-skid metal flooring, great. She relatched the box and dragged it perpendicular to the wall of crates. Slowly, she rearranged the stack into a three-sided makeshift fort.

Almost cozy.

The door hissed open, loud and clunky.

Frankie tensed and stood quickly. She could see over the now-shorter stack of crates.

Huxley Parker, pulling a cart heavy with security microphones and sleek microcams. His shirt was a little less crisp than earlier in the day, his copper hair a bit mussed, but that ridiculous fancy wine-colored jacket was made of stronger stuff. The button of the neural implant at his temple was dim.

He didn't look surprised to see her.

"Nice," he said, eyeing her crude fort and stroking his beard as if judging it architecturally. His cologne, now faint, could not quite mask a nervous flop-sweat. "Planning to defend the quantum box from ghosts?"

"Pirates," Frankie said drily, resisting the urge to roll her eyes. "Just keeping my toes from falling off."

He smiled and shook his head. Moving briskly around the device, he slapped cams carelessly into place at each corner of the table. "Pointless, you know. If anything happens, it'll be remotely triggered. Sleep here if you must—nobody's gonna be tip-toeing dramatically through those doors."

She folded her arms stubbornly. "Keep the cameras off me. I snore."

Parker laughed, his low tenor echoing in the cavernous bay. "No promises. You heard Scarlet. Footage from every angle." He headed toward the far wall and used the cargo boxes as a ladder to set up more cameras.

Moments later, another figure slipped through the open doorway. Tala Foss, curls wild, eyes wilder. She beelined for the transmitter.

"I had to see—is it really working? Power draw, relay methodology—" She stopped short, and dropped to one knee.

"Is that—an Orr box?" Her voice dropped to a frightened

whisper. "We could run the whole lab off that thing for a month!" She looked up at Frankie. "How did it get here?"

Frankie shrugged, watching Parker out of the corner of her eye as he moved down the bay. He reached out to set a camera on top of a pile of crates, and then pulled back fast.

Spike jumped down from the pile, and sauntered toward Frankie.

Tala, her tablet out, was taking some kind of readings while sticking close to the space heater when Lee Calavera strode in. Their augmented lenses caught the icy-blue end of the light spectrum. Frankie sighed. This was not making her job easier.

"Parker," Calavera barked, cold. "The cameras are supposed to cover the entire area, not just the entrance. Center axis, please."

Parker straightened, rolling his neck. "I'm aware, Lee. You want to do it yourself?"

Ignoring Parker, Calavera rounded sharply on Tala, their voice pure steel. "Foss, you are not authorized to be here. If you must gawk, do it via the remote feed."

Tala winced, hugged her tablet and headed immediately for the door. "Sorry, I just—" She vanished out into the corridor.

Calavera sighed, pinched the bridge of their nose, and stalked off to re-check the placement of the cams. Parker trailed behind them with an air of wounded dignity. Eventually the pair left, their bickering faded down the hall, and the storage bay felt cavernous again.

And dark, but for the glow of the heater and the little yellow lantern from Frankie's backpack.

Frankie leaned back against her now-much-thinner pack, exhaling. Spike padded over to join her. The cyvlossic placed her very furry self, which could keep her warm even in the vacuum of space, between Frankie and the heater.

Not a chance. Frankie pulled Spike to her side. The cyvlossic could share some of that warmth.

A moment later, Spike's ears flicked up, and then settled down. Frankie heard the softest of footfalls.

Tala stepped into the light of the heater, clutching a carafe and two black ceramic mugs, their printed designs nearly worn off. Her cheeks were pink.

"I, uh, didn't want to leave you alone. So cold. So I brought? Some tea I made… with my garden. If you want?"

Frankie grinned and patted the slice of space on her other side. They could make a heat sandwich.

Tala settled comfortably between Frankie and the wall of her three-sided fort. She poured each of them a mug of tea, handing one to Frankie. Their jackets shushed as they brushed each other.

Cozy.

For a few minutes, they sat quietly, sipping the tea and listening to the semi-random crackle of the space heater. Frankie could feel her toes again.

Frankie looked into her cup. "Is there mint in here? I love mint."

"Yes, peppermint!" Tala said. "And chamomile, and lemongrass. No honey, of course, so I used lemon."

Spike nudged over, sniffing at the cup. And then sniffing deeper. The cyvlossic shook her head, and stepped a paw that seemed to hold all her mighty weight onto—into—Frankie's thigh to get closer to the cup.

And then sniffed again.

Frankie bumped Spike off her thigh and back over to her own side. "Get your own cup."

"You know," Tala said shyly, "I used to dream about places like this. Not—" she gestured around at the stacked crates and illegal tech— "not exactly this. But somewhere I could think, and nobody was demanding miracles, or telling me what was forbidden, or…" Her voice caught. "People in my family lived in a commune—some would call it a cult, I guess. Everything was 'for the benefit of all.' Here, for all the pressure, at least I can think about myself. Sometimes."

Frankie watched Tala, the way she traced the rim of her mug with her thumb. "What do you dream about now?"

Tala smiled, small but genuine. "Freedom. Real freedom. A ship of my own, maybe. Something small. Or a garden—a big one, not just boxes and grow lights—where nobody tells me what can grow."

Frankie clinked her mug against Tala's. "To gardens, and escape pods."

Tala smiled warmly, genuine and unexpectedly vulnerable.

Spike rested her chin on Frankie's thigh. Tala reached hesitantly toward Spike.

"May I? Touch her?"

"Up to Spike." But it looked like the cyvlossic had been angling for that all along.

Tala stroked the cyvlossic with reverence. Spike accepted the adoration with regal grace.

"She's... incredible," Tala said, stroking Spike's sleek head. "I wish I'd had someone like her growing up."

Spike's ears snapped forward. Was that a faint scritching sound? Tala startled, and then scratched at the cotton of her cargo pants. That must have been it.

Spike nuzzled closer, warmth and calm radiating off her solid frame. The cyvlossic sighed herself into her sleep breathing. Better than a antiseptic apartment blanket.

Frankie took another sip of tea, suddenly proud, suddenly homesick.

Suddenly, really sick.

She couldn't keep her eyes open. The heat was too much.

She had to lie down, right now.

Food poisoning?

But she didn't feel sick. Just so, so sleepy.

She set the empty mug down. Tala swept it up, and scooted a bit away so Frankie could lay down. The backpack was surprisingly comfortable under her head.

"Sweet dreams," Tala said, breathless voice misting in the cold.

Frankie's last sight, before her eyes drifted closed and would not open, was Spike, more relaxed than she had ever seen her.

CHAPTER
TWENTY-TWO

FOR A LONG, aching moment, Frankie hovered in the twilight between sleep and waking. Time had collapsed into meaningless echoes, blurred by lingering cold seeping from the hard floor of the cargo bay and the scratchy curve of the backpack under her head. A bitter aftertaste clung to her tongue, thick, sour, familiar.

Someone had knocked her out, again? First Prakara Gold's poison gas, and now this.

This mission sucked.

She smacked dry lips. Musky, like dirty socks.

Valerian. In the tea?

She'd been drugged.

Her eyes snapped open painfully, gummy lashes sticking. Harsh, pricking cold assaulted her face and neck. Outside the weak orange glow of the battered space heater in front of her, everything else was midnight shadows.

Spike was beside her. Tense and huge in the darkness. Her muscles tight, her whole body vibrating as if to say, "get up, get up, get up!"

Frankie lurched upright, adrenaline punching through the cobwebs of sleep. Her body yowled in protest, cramped from sleeping on the floor. In the cold. She squinted against an almost unbearable ache behind her eyes and fumbled for her lantern, ice cold.

Some sentinel she made.

When she flicked it on, the circle of light was blinding in the cargo bay's cave-darkness. The air burned with a frozen, metallic sharpness.

She swept the beam forward.

The quantum box still sat on its square metal table.

But all the power cables had been disconnected. Dropped to the floor like a web broken by a broom.

Frankie's heart froze. Then cracked at the edges with reluctant suspicion.

Tala.

How had she known how to take the box offline?

Because she'd built it.

Shit.

Why? What had Tala said last night? Something about a cult? An everybody cult?

Frankie couldn't remember. But at least the danger had passed, for today. If the box was dormant, it wouldn't be able to interfere with the big Central District test.

But something wasn't right.

The little control panel on the box still glowed. It was still on?

Cold dread pooled in Frankie's gut.

She swept the light down to the Orr box. Someone had plugged the quantum box in. Using a cable that looked like a ship's tether, it was so wide.

Outer-rim tech.

The danger had not passed.

Spike pawed at the cable, toe beans out. No joy.

Frankie set the lantern down and clawed numbly through her coat pocket. She pulled out her White Moon tablet, barely able to see the screen through the blur of panic. Her trembling fingers nearly dropped it. A frantic swipe, a stutter—the security app loaded.

Ten camera feeds. All but one black squares filled with featureless midnight-blue static. The tenth showed Frankie, lit from below by the faint orange of the little heater.

No infrared view, no night vision. Nothing.

Great job, Parker…" she muttered, voice cracked dry. Huxley Parker would make a bad spy.

Or a good one.

She toggled back. Video logs played in crisp, loud, full-color loop: Frankie, Spike, and Tala, laughing quietly in their fort; Parker and Lee squabbling about camera placement. No sign of Tala leaving. No sign of anyone else coming in. Nothing after the lights went out, except this endless replay of safety.

Clever.

Sharp panic roared in her chest. What the hell had really happened?

Spike nudged her, pressing the heavy arc of her skull into the back of Frankie's knee. A wake-up call, a warning, a comfort.

Frankie bent down and pressed her cold forehead to Spike's warm fur, breathing deep. She forced her mind to work. They could puzzle out the why's later. Now they needed to act.

She activated the comm-link to Gold, throat raw, voice shaking: "Quantum box tampered. Plugged into Orr. Power's completely rerouted—"

Prakara Gold's response blasted through, shrill and frantic against her ear: "What?! Unlock it NOW! You have no idea—The countdown's started—fifteen minutes! Move! Get here immediately!" Frankie could picture the woman pacing the lab in silk and venom, already calculating disaster and blame.

Frankie's lantern beam outlined that thick cable—a brutal twist-lock, neatly executed. Secure and immovable, a trick she'd seen only in ships. Needed a special tool to unlock it.

She had one.

Up on the Spear.

She felt sick, cold, betrayed.

Frankie gulped cold air, her breath turning to fog, and scrambled for her pack. She slung it over one shoulder. Spike circled once rapidly—checking crates, checking shadows—and dashed soundlessly toward the double doors to the main corridor.

Frankie bolted after her, legs aching brutally. She pounded feet across the echoing cargo bay and out into the corridor. Down the curve, and another turn, toward the tube that led to the Commons. Corridor walls blurred; everything lit by only emergency lights.

"Lights on!" Frankie shouted at her tablet, and at the walls. No love.

She slammed painfully into a corner turning too fast, hip meeting metal locker with bruising accuracy. Frankie barely registered the pain. Now they were in the corridor to the Commons.

Spike loped fluidly ahead, on silent paws, guiding her through the semi-darkness.

Frankie nearly sobbed, frustration tearing ragged breaths, pulse hammering:

How had she trusted Tala? What had Tala seen—known— done?

No answers.

No time.

They raced through the little patch of the Central Commons and into the corridor to the quantum lab. Frankie was slowing.

Push on, just a little more.

Ahead, the quantum lab's pressure door was slowly closing.

Spike shot forward and through on a growl. Frankie lunged, managing to get a hand and leg through. The door paused, letting the rest of her slip through. Then it closed and latched, sealing everyone in.

TWENTY-THREE

FRANKIE BURST through the door into the quantum lab just before it closed and sealed itself ahead of the big experiment. The refrigerator chill, gently curving lab felt toasty after spending half a night passed out in Cargo Bay 12-C. And her heaving breaths didn't make mist.

The lab was buzzing. No longer quiet and controlled, but sun-bright—and vibrating at the fevered edge of chaos.

Or discovery.

Screens scrolled urgent-looking data. Frantic fingers pulled at the edges of holograms or pounded floating keyboards. Wint barked out orders that in the time it took to get to the high arched ceiling and back had been modified by Gold, and then again by Wint.

Under the high white dome, scientists and techs swarmed the consoles—Scarlett, Tala, Calavera, Parker, even Marsh, over by the inner window-wall—all pulled taut by a collective, desperate urgency.

The heart of the flurry, at the back of the room, behind that floor-to-ceiling window, the original quantum transmitter rested on its table. Even it was caught up in the chaos, it's once-quiet casing now pulsing insistently with bright blue indicator bars. Frankie could hear its floor-shaking thrum. Power collecting, barely leashed.

Scarlett, in a fresh labcoat that matched the golden red of her hair, stood stiff-backed at the console next to Huxley Parker's. Her hand holding an oversized earpiece to her ear, her eyes on what looked like the transmitter box, only its metal table was black, not gray.

Jin Wint couldn't seem to keep her head still. Her attention snapped from one of her six floating consoles to another. Who knew how much she had going on inside those AR glasses, as well. Wint muttered what sounded like checklist items—or an agitated prayer.

Tala Foss shadowed her, looking like she was trying to guess what Wint would need next. The young engineer looked frazzled and excited, a mirror image of Wint.

Marsh prowled the inner wall, where backup servers and other tech was corralled. Parker called confirmations culled from rapidly blinking network readouts, seeming cool. But his usual cedar scent overlaid by sharp, anxious sweat.

Lee Calavera stood by the window to the transmitter, just looking at it. Or, more likely, processing the feed from their implants.

In the center stood Prakara Gold, royal purple silk-clad arms crossed tight over her chest, snarling at Jin Wint and everyone else. Telling them to double-check the field stabilizers stability fields or something.

Spike was sniffing around Calavera, trying to get into the room with the transmitter box. She looked for all the world like she was hunting a rat.

Well, weren't they all.

When Gold saw Frankie, her eyes narrowed to dark, angry

slits. Frankie skidded to a halt beside the gilt, glowering Gold. Frankie set her backpack down next to a table leg, out of the way, and glanced up at the countdown on the main display.

02:57.

"Did you unplug the traitor's quantum box?" Gold said.

Frankie swallowed through a raw, aching throat. "Yeah, no."

"WHAT?" Gold's eyebrows crashed like thunderclouds.

Parker turned around to look at her.

"There's no sign of power drain," he said.

"It was unplugged from the siphons," Frankie said, still huffing and puffing at an embarrassing rate. "But now it's hooked to the Orr box. Locked on. I don't have the tool to unlock it."

Pure horror flashed across Gold's sharp features.

In front of her, Wint's voice rang suddenly loud, trying for calm but sounding desperate. "Quantum handshake confirmed."

"I need to talk to Tala," Frankie said.

Tala, next to Wint, went still, but didn't look at Frankie.

"She pulled the plug—" Frankie started.

"Later," Wint cut in, her AR glasses a rainbow of color. How could she even see through that to look at the array of screens in front of her. "Focus, everyone! Pulse alignment active."

"Channel secure," Parker said. "Central District is receiving."

"Don't let her touch anything!" Frankie said.

"Nobody touch anything!" Wint shouted back. "Transmission initiating—now."

The room collectively inhaled. For a heartbeat, silence. Then the quantum box released a delicate, hauntingly musical note. A frequency both beautiful and deeply unsettling, like crystal chimes shattering beneath water.

On the floating display in front of Scarlett, a stark graphic blinked to life. Two dots, far apart on the screen. "White Moon: Sending" pulsed blue; the distant "Central: Receiving" blinked white. Frankie's skin prickled, anxiety itching under all the layers of her clothes.

White Moon's dot went white. Central's didn't change.

Wasn't this transmission supposed to be instantaneous?

Huxley Parker piped up, "Chief, I've got Central voice. Video soon."

Scarlett nodded. She tapped the comm in her ear. "Central, this is White Moon. Confirm receipt. Please."

The comm crackled, so sharp it made Frankie jump. A woman's voice, calm and professional, filtered into the lab: "Central here. Stand by. Processing your packet."

They waited. A second… two… three…

Scarlett's features tightened visibly with growing panic, her fingers digging deeper against her comm earpiece. Wint closed her eyes in silent dread, her AR glasses going dim.

Something was wrong.

The voice from Central returned, confusion obvious beneath the practiced professionalism.

"White Moon. We're reading an anomaly. Your payload—it's particulate. Dust, or ash?"

Gasps. Wint's hand flew to her mouth. Tala blurted out, "No way—the stabilization matrix was clean!"

"Central." Scarlett shouted over everyone. "Please send video. Internal camera view." She pointed at her screen and looked at Parker. "Here."

After another teeth-grinding five-second delay, the receiving end's image came through. Parker projected it onto the screen in front of Scarlett.

Everyone crowded the screen.

The Central District's quantum transmission chamber, a hermetically-sealed cube, looked empty but for a shallow ceramic receiving dish at the center. It should look like that. They were sending a nanobot, which wouldn't be visible to humans without magnification. Scarlett wasn't thinking straight.

Frankie looked closer. On the dish, a gray smear. Charred, gritty residue.

Frankie's pulse staggered.

Like soot.

Like something small, alive, burned to nothing.

She pressed a palm to her chest. She had to catch her breath.

"Not possible!" Wint's voice shook with horror. "The payload was code. We switched out the bot for pure patterned data. Taking no chances. How could it—"

Scarlett demanded, "Run diagnostics—someone's swapped the payload! Did you see anything? Read anything? Anything at all?"

"If someone intercepted," Wint's brows were almost in her eyes. "What did they send?"

"Whatever was in that blasted pirate transmitter," Gold said.

"That looked like that?"

Frankie's memory flipped back. The scritch, scritch, in the cargo bay last night, its echo this morning.

A mouse? On an airless moon?

Her stomach twisted again, acid-high, mouth dry and bitter. She cast a desperate glance at Spike, still sitting next to the glass wall.

Spike nodded once, slow and grave.

Gold's voice, low, awful: "Someone just proved we can send living matter… and kill it."

A cold horror fell upon the room.

For a long minute, everyone stood still, eyes unfocused. Some were probably bitterly reviewing every step of the process, others gloomily predicting what kind of dark future loomed. One, Frankie hoped, was feeling guilty.

Jan Wint sank heavily onto a too-tall stool, curling inward, hugging herself. Head bowed dangerously low, breaths ragged.

Prakara Gold stared fixedly at nothing, eyes burning black with fury, betrayal—and genuine confusion.

Scarlett Bulwarion stared blankly at the the live feed from Central, face bloodlessly pale beneath her carefully styled auburn hair. Lee Calavera watched Scarlett, grim. Ready to catch their suddenly-vulnerable chief if she collapsed.

Marsh crouched by Spike, her eyes narrowed dangerously, glaring at Parker.

Huxley Parker ran his hands through his hair, then clasped them behind his neck and stretched back a little. He stared at the ceiling as if he wished he could rocket far away.

Tala Foss, pale and grim, stared at the door to the hallway, now automatically opening.

And then ran for it.

CHAPTER
TWENTY-FOUR

RUNNING, again.

Frankie's feet pounded painfully against corridor flooring, echoes whipping behind her like snapping ghosts. Ahead, Tala Foss sprinted desperately, her gray coveralls flapping, her blond curls wild behind her.

Spike moved like fluid lightning at Frankie's flank—a black-and-gray-striped blur passing her on silent haunches.

Cargo Bay 12-C loomed suddenly ahead, its open doors spilling white brilliance into the corridor. Tala plunged through without slowing, Spike at her heels.

Huxley Parker came up from behind Frankie, face set and pale, not even breathing hard. He caught her eye briefly before they both charged into the bay.

The scene of the crime.

Frankie's jury-rigged fort sat stubbornly in the middle of the cavernous bay; it seemed smaller now, under the high-bright ceiling lights. Just a squat three walls of stacked white-and-orange Skoll shipping crates. Beyond it, exposed on its square metal table, the pirate quantum transmitter.

Which, they all now knew, worked like a charm.

But they didn't see Tala.

They didn't stop running.

"Tala, stop!" Scarlett Bulwarion's voice sang out, sharp, her silhouette framed in the doorway. A rush of others spilled in behind her. Lee Calavera, face calm, breathing hard. Jin Wint, running on fumes and fury. Prakara Gold, glittering, not running but somehow arriving nearly even with the rest of them. The bay felt suddenly crowded, air sharp and bitter, an arena waiting for a match.

They found Tala kneeling by the Orr box, tugging hard at the thick, locked cable tethering it to her illicit transmitter. She saw them, her face rictus panic, and tugged harder.

"It won't come out!" she said.

Parker surged forward, shoving Tala roughly aside. She fell back, landing with a startled cry inside Frankie's makeshift fort. One of her hands knocked over the battered space heater Frankie had forgotten to shut off.

Spike leaped gracefully onto the crate-fort wall behind Tala, eyes fierce, tense body glaring threat.

By the time Tala was on her feet, scowling at Parker, Scarlett had reached the group. Scarlett stood beside Parker, back to the illicit transmitter, blocking Tala within the boxes. Parker loomed over Tala, a hawk with a curly-haired mouse in its sights.

Frankie made way for Lee Calavera, who took Parker's other side. Scarlett's assistant was officially in charge of security here.

Marsh, face grim, scar livid, breathing hard, leaned on the outside of the fort's back wall, closest to the hallway door, her arms crossed and resting on the lid of one of the top cargo boxes. She did not seem to notice Spike's tail flashing back and forth next to her shoulder; all her attention was on Tala.

Wint ignored Tala entirely and went to the square metal table. She lifted a hand to adjust her fancy glasses and stared hard at the transmitter. Gold joined her; she put a hand on top of the transmitter as if to see if it was still warm.

If they even got warm, Frankie didn't know.

The bay delivery doors, far to the rear of everyone, heavy and armored, were sealed. But the sense of exposure was total.

Tala sagged against a crate, looking impossibly small.

Scarlett's voice rang hard in the chill. "Tell me everything."

"I didn't do anything!" Tala's pale face had gone blotchy, even in this chill, but her eyes burned.

Scarlett's voice tightened, each word a blow. "You built an unauthorized quantum device. That you stole power for."

"Nobody would listen! I thought if I just made the thing, then people would have to see."

"See what?" Scarlett said. "That you have no respect for the work of your teammates?"

Before Tala could reply, Wint snorted. "She didn't build this. She's an assistant."

"See?" Tala pleaded to Scarlett.

Scarlett huffed a puff cloud of frustration into the chilled air. She looked over her shoulder at Wint.

"So, if she didn't build it, who did? You?"

Wint stiffened. "Poor joke, Bulwarion."

"Then look at the facts, Wint." Scarlett's attention snapped back to Tala. The junior quantum engineer wilted under her glare.

"No, I did it. I did it alone—except Parker helped me with the logs. At least, he said he was helping." Tears welled, but she blinked them away. "I just wanted to show it could be done. No more secrets. All the worlds deserve good tech, not just the high councils or corporate buyers."

She glared at Parker "I thought you believed in open science."

"Open science?" Scarlett's frown darkened dangerously. "You stole power—you sabotaged everything we've worked for—out of your idea of open science?"

Tala shook her head, desperate. "No! I wanted the tests to work. The power loss at each node was minuscule. It harmed nothing. I would never hurt anyone—not even a mouse."

"Right," Parker said, disbelief in the twist of his mouth.

Tala turned to him. "I thought you were my friend. I thought—"

"She's lying," Parker said. He took a step toward Tala, who tried to shrink back, but her back was already against the crates. Spike, above Tala, went on alert, her eyes on Parker.

Scarlett gestured for silence, her breath trailing in the cold. "Let her finish."

"I thought…" Tala's energy faded. She looked at her hands, as if they had betrayed her. "I thought the world should be fair."

Scarlett eased back, confusion on her face.

A tap on the table behind them caught everyone's attention. Gold's nails clicked impatiently on the Orr box. "And this? How exactly did a junior scientist manage to pick up a virtually unlimited power supply?"

Tala looked down, her voice dropping to a desperate whisper. She wrung her hands so tightly Frankie winced. "I didn't," she said. "Last month the Orr box—it just appeared. Unattached, unexplained. I had no clue how or why. So I ignored it."

Gold stared at her, eyes wide. "You ignored it? An almost-endless power supply?" She glanced at Scarlett, another question in her eyes.

"We never took delivery of an Orr box," Calavera interrupted. They touched the implant at their temple, as if to remind everyone that they could search files on the fly. "And if we did, we'd never toss it into an unused storage bay."

Scarlett's tone hardened to ice. "Whoever plugged your transmitter directly into it last night begs to differ."

"It wasn't me!" Tala's voice, always thin, was going reedy. "After Frankie fell asleep—"

"After you *drugged* me," Frankie cut in. "And Spike!"

"Well, yes, sorry. But not a lot, and totally plant-based. I just needed an hour." Tala shook her head, getting back to the point. "Then, I unplugged my machine. I pulled every cord. When I left it last night, it was dead."

"It's alive now," Wint said. She kicked the Orr box gently. "Hard-wired. I suppose you don't have the wrench-key to unplug it with you, do you?"

"I never had it." Tala's voice was gossamer. "You have to believe me."

Wint shook her head. "Quite the magic trick."

"Not magic," Frankie said. Another piece had fallen into place. "It's money. Skoll money."

Parker flinched, but tried to cover it by stroking his coppery beard. "Skoll? The shippers? Why?"

Lee Calavera looked interested. "Yes, why?"

"Marsh." Frankie waved toward the engineer. "She traced the transmissions. Every clandestine message that left here was headed to known Skoll hubs."

"The crates," Scarlett murmured, gaze shifting to the stacks around them. "This entire bay is Skoll containers."

Calavera nodded. "We rotate trade boxes. Someone ships us full, we return empties."

"The Orr box must have been smuggled in tucked into a Skoll crate," Frankie said. "Easy enough when they're all identical."

"Right under our noses," Scarlett groaned. Then her expression went blank.

Then Calavera's, and Wint's.

A message, coming in.

"It really was a mouse," Scarlett said. She put a palm to her forehead. "Central tested it. They're asking if we checked the box beforehand."

Wint rolled her eyes. "A damn mouse." She set her hands on

her hips and glared past Scarlett to Tala. "Your put a damned mouse in your box."

Next to Wint, Gold shivered. Her peach silk sari and sweater set was pale protection from the cold. She sidled up to Scarlett, and put an arm around her waist. Scarlett leaned into her.

"Better they think it's an accident than sabotage," Gold said.

"But I didn't do it." Tala, voice soft and flat, stared down at her twisted hands. Giving up.

Spike sent Frankie a message, text only. Frankie pulled it up.

A receipt. For mouse chow.

To Huxley Parker.

Interesting.

"Parker," Frankie turned to him. "Enjoy keeping mice as pets?"

Everyone swung toward Parker. He flushed under the scrutiny but straightened indignantly. "Pets, yes. Harmless, legal pets!"

Then, as if he couldn't help himself, he looked down.

So did everyone else.

Tucked in the shadows of the under-shelf holding the Orr box was an object. Something metal, and flat.

Frankie pulled it out. Unfolded it.

A portable mouse cage.

"Calavera," Scarlett said. "Where was Parker last night?"

"Here," Calavera said. "We all saw him." They looked at Parker. "Didn't see any mouse."

"Of course not!" Parker's face went red, then white. "You think I'd risk my career for this?" he spat, but the words collapsed in the vast space. "You're all just looking for a scapegoat."

Scarlett's eyes narrowed. "We have a scapegoat. We're looking for the criminal."

Calavera lifted a finger, data scrolling past their eyes.

"Yes," they said. "Hall camera views. After Parker and I left, Foss returned. Then Foss left, and Parker came in a minute later."

As if he'd been waiting for Tala to leave.

"Tala," Marsh said. "Parker helped you with the logs, you said. Did he help with the power siphoning, as well?"

Tala glared at Parker. "He said it's a network, and that's his specialty. He even came with me, once or twice."

Marsh glanced at Calavera. "Bet I can guess which junctions."

The ones with the transmitters.

Parker's hand went to the pocket in his fancy coat. He stilled it before it could plunge in.

Interesting.

"Got a fancy Orr box conduit key in that pocket, Parker?" Frankie said.

Understanding rippled visibly among the group.

And anger.

Parker's arrogance buckled. He sagged from his hips.

Tala straightened herself up. Her tear-soft eyes went hard.

"You killed an innocent creature to frame me? Me—raised in Amity Village, who believe 'First, do no harm.' Parker! Why?"

"Yes, Huxley," Scarlett said, tilting her head. "Why?"

No denial came. Parker's shoulders slumped; his voice turned bitter, cornered. "Why not? Skoll offered more credits than Central District ever dreamed. I could finally get my implants fixed."

He scratched his temple behind the implant. "Tala said her prototype worked. She couldn't stop talking about it. Sent something to the moon! Had to hide that one."

Gold, still tucked next to Scarlett, gasped. "It does work."

"Stupid girl couldn't stop swearing me to secrecy." Parker rolled on. "But she wasn't going to show you until after today's big test. So we had a window. The Skolls agreed the insertion test worked, but they wanted real proof." He shrugged, not convincingly. "So I gave it to them."

He glared at Tala. "Except no, it doesn't work."

Now Tala's tears started to flow. "You did this all for money?"

"To get rid of the damn headaches! Besides, if shipping could be revolutionized, why shouldn't I benefit?"

"But information should be free!"

"Sure, Tala. Like that was ever going to work."

Wint's voice broke in, cold, raw, and bitter.

"So the Skolls know every blessed detail of our work." She glared through her fancy blinking glasses at Scarlett. "So much for giving up my life to sit out here in some stinking moon base because that's the only way to keep things locked down."

She took her glasses off. Her eyes looked smaller, and very tired. "You've destroyed everything, anyway. Central will close us down for sure. We're finished."

Prakara Gold, for once, had no comeback.

"That's tomorrow's problem," Scarlett said. Her voice sliced icy-quick between them, authority absolute. "Today, we consider Huxley Parker."

Parker's eyes flicked to the far door, calculating. For a heartbeat, Frankie thought she saw the same wild panic she'd seen in Tala minutes ago. This time, though, no one was going to give Parker the benefit of the doubt.

He spun toward the exit, desperate. Took two running steps before Scarlett or Frankie thought to grab at him.

But Marsh was already moving, interception written in the fierce line of her shoulders. Spike, too—a silent streak of muscle and fur—dropped like a backpack on Parker, claws out.

Parker winced, trapped not by walls but by the weight of every eye upon him. And a cyvlossic.

Lee Calavera stepped past Scarlett, voice impossibly calm. "Don't make this harder, Parker."

Parker started to deflate. His hand hovered uncertainly over his coat pocket. But Marsh's grip landed heavy on his shoulder. He staggered, caught, half-bowing under the pressure. His bravado was gone, replaced now with something brittle and small.

Scarlett moved in, palm open. "Your badge. Tablet. That key. All of it. Now."

Parker hesitated, some last, stubborn part of his pride refusing to let go. The skin around his implants looked bruised.

Spike kicked him near his kidneys, launching herself off his back and onto the floor.

His hands trembling, Parker pulled free his badge, data tablet, wristcom, and the little wrench-key that had changed everything. One after another, the tokens of status and sabotage piled up in Scarlett's outstretched hand.

The silence was absolute.

His defeat, total.

Scarlett's voice twisted the knife. "You're finished, Parker. Lee, lock him out. Marsh, see that he stays away from every critical console."

"Done," Lee replied instantly, eyes on Parker. "Come with me."

With a final, ugly glare, Parker tried to shake Marsh off—but her grip only tightened, steering him firmly toward the hall. He lingered there for a moment, a shadow of the man he had tried to be—then vanished into the hall, Marsh a silent, unyielding escort. Behind them, Calavera an implacable shadow.

"We'll put him in his room," Calavera said. "No net access."

Spike bumped against Frankie's hip with a little chirp-smirk, ears twitching smugly.

CHAPTER
TWENTY-FIVE

ONCE MARSH, Parker, and Calavera were through the bay doors and out of view, a heavy stillness fell across the group. All eyes turned toward Tala.

Scarlett took a step toward her, leaving Gold and Frankie behind. Tala pressed herself against a crate, knuckles white, her wild curls haloed in the harsh overhead light.

"Tala Foss," Scarlett said, "You risked everything—our work, the team, the mission—for your ideals. However sincere they may be, they do not excuse your actions. You broke protocol, stole power, endangered lives, and severely damaged our reputation."

Tala swallowed hard, lips trembling. She didn't flinch from Scarlett's gaze, though—just nodded once, the weight of her guilt settling over her shoulders.

"I'm sorry, Chief," she scratched out. "For the lies. The stealing. For letting anyone doubt the safety of our work. I... just ... I didn't know how else to—"

Scarlett raised a hand, cutting her off. "No more," she said, voice gentle but implacable. "Go to your apartment. Pack your things. You'll be leaving on the same shuttle we find for Parker."

"And don't expect a glowing reference, Wint said, bitter, not even looking at Tala.

Tala's body fold inward like a house of cards collapsing in slow motion. Her spine curved forward, shoulders rolling until she was nearly doubled over against the crate. Her legs gave out just enough that she slid down a few inches, the rough metal catching on her overalls, bunching the fabric at her hips.

Understanding moved across her face like a slow-motion wave. Her brow furrowed first, as if she were trying to solve an impossible equation. Then her eyes widened—not in surprise, but in that terrible moment of comprehension. Her mouth opened slightly, forming a soundless "oh" that never quite emerged.

Her curls drooped as her head tilted downward. Under the harsh overhead lights, she looked like a wilted flower, all the fight drained out of her.

"Now get out of here," Scarlett said.

Tala pushed herself off the crate with trembling hands, her movements smooth but hollow, like a ghost going through the motions. She sidled past Frankie without seeing her, her steps efficient but empty. Slowly, she headed for the door.

Scarlett and the others had already turned away, back to the transmitter on the table behind them. Their voices carried across the cargo bay as if Tala had already vanished.

Wint stared bleakly at the transmitter. "Central will close us down for sure," she repeated, softer, sadder. "We're done."

Scarlett pressed her lips together. "You know Skolls would snatch us up. We could take their offer—"

Gold shook her head before she could finish. "Even if we could move cargo—hell, if we could move a grape—Skolls want control, not partnership. Bad deal for us. And the schematics aren't even there. Nanobots getting through once is a fluke, not a promise."

Tala stopped halfway to the door. She turned to look back at them, and took a shaky breath. Still working the problem.

"Go, Tala," Scarlett said without looking back.

Tala's shoulders sagged. She turned back toward the door and kept walking.

Scarlett almost smiled, but weariness won. She took Gold's hand in hers. "So we let Central think we have a mouse problem? It's the least dangerous truth."

"Safest," Gold agreed, though her expression implied gentle mockery. Her bangles flashed as she swept the issue away. "But maybe not for long—think bigger, Scar. Skolls might bite. They're on the hook already. But Konrad Orr, his bite is bigger."

Everyone in the bay flinched at the name—the shadow of a man with too much reach and too little mercy.

"Orr…" Scarlett actually seemed to be considering it. "He already funds another lab here. Already has clearance." She shook her head, not quite convinced.

Wint snorted, a puff in the chilled air. "Orr's a meddler. Nobody wants him looking over their shoulder."

Amen to that.

Gold looked back, checking that Tala had gone.

"Scar," she said, "we can't let that girl go."

"We can." Scarlett voice did not leave space to argue. Except to one who was used to arguing with it.

"Take a minute," Gold said. "Tala's mistakes are her own— but so are ours, for letting such a rare mind drown in red tape and silence." She shot a pointed glare at Wint, who looked away, jaw stiff.

"But more importantly," she said, tapping the transmitter. "Once she's loose, the Skolls will scoop her up."

"She'd never work for them," Scarlett said.

"They're not above blackmail. They'd steal her family, or her child. Or her." Gold shuddered so hard her bangles tinkled. "They tried to steal me, once."

No wonder Prakara Gold traveled with poison gas.

"And if not the Skolls, someone else. The girl's a dreamer," Gold shook her head. "And a quantum genius. How long do you think she'll last out there?"

Scarlett pursed her lips. But then shook her head. "She's lost our trust."

Wint huffed. "I, for one, never want to see her again. A mouse!"

"It wasn't her mouse, Jin." Gold's voice somehow carried an eye roll.

"I'm serious!" Wint pushed her glasses up. "I will not work with her. Ever. Again."

Frankie unplugged the space heater. It had done yeoman work. She stepped over to Spike. This seemed like an in-house conversation. "Should we go?" she whispered to her friend.

But Spike was alert, on her haunches, watching the three around the transmitter. As if they were a drama show or something.

"You want her? Take her back with you, then," Wint said. "Learn how to mentor, if you can."

Scarlett was lifting a hand, as if to call a time out, but Gold merely smiled.

"Well, Jin, I've been thinking about that. You hate it out here, and I'm falling in love with it again." She smiled—actually smiled—at Scarlett. "I'm thinking of staying."

Scarlett smiled back, as if Prakara Gold was the only person in the room. "I think we might come to some sort of accommodation on this.

"Probation," Gold said. "Before Tala starts, she spends some time in her room She writes everything—every power hack and shortcut and method—down for Marsh. A full technical report on the siphoning. A detailed report for myself and Wint on the transmitter. And the Orr box."

"Should take her some time," Wint muttered. "More than she deserves."

Gold nodded to Wint like a queen accepting her due.

Scarlett's face went blank for a second. "Parker is under confinement, system access locked down. Once the Skoll cargo ship arrives, we hand him over. But we're keeping the Orr box."

"What Orr box?" Gold said.

"Exactly." Scarlett grimaced. "I can't imagine Parker's new bosses throwing him a welcome party. But at least he'll be off our hands—and on someone else's leash."

"Skoll ship?" Frankie shot a startled glance at Spike.

"Due in three days or so, Lee says." Scarlett tapped her lips. "I thought it odd timing, so soon since the last one. Guess now we know why?"

Frankie glanced at Spike, back up top of the little fort. Why did the Skolls always seem to find them where they should not be?

They couldn't stay to see how the politics played out—not with Skoll eyes about to sweep the station. Not with her own cargo ledger trailing behind her like a guilty conscience.

She had to get back to the lab. Grab her backpack. Get out of here.

Scarlett glanced over, noting Frankie's movement. "Captain? You planning to be here when Skoll's customs team starts snooping around?"

Frankie shook her head, words catching in her dry throat. "Think we'll be scarce by then."

Scarlett's mouth twitched. "Probably for the best. As far as I'm concerned, you were never here."

"Thank you, Chief." Frankie's relief twined with regret. She liked Scarlett. And she really wanted to see what Tala would do next.

But she'd be glad to be free of Prakara Gold.

Gold gave her a little jingle-arm salute. "Next time you need a trade reference, don't mention today."

Frankie slipped toward the exit, Spike leading the way. The doors whispered closed behind them.

Time for them to jump.

CHAPTER
TWENTY-SIX

FRANKIE LEANED against the open entry to the Spear's kitchen.

Home.

After all the frigid corridors, sterile guest rooms, and cargo crates that screamed "Skoll," this cozy, softly-lit spot felt like coming out of an ice storm and slipping into a warm bath.

The ship—her ship, the Spear—smelled of industrial soap, sun-bright coffee, and just a hint of peanut sauce from last night's attempt at stir fry. Somewhere, a panel buzzed in the wall; she'd have to get to that.

She had the time, now.

Everything was a little too clean. A couple of Scarlett's lab-issue supply bots had come up with her in the elevator and, after dropping their packages here in the kitchen, traveled up and down the corridors and open rooms all morning, sorting, tidying, rearranging. Nice thought, but Frankie had had to talk Ship down from zapping them all to oblivion.

Ship kept the place very clean, very nice, everyone agreed.

Frankie had just sent the short report to SystA:

Incident resolved. Key personnel accounted for. Tech secured, but has the strong interest of the Skolls and, potentially, Konrad Orr. Recommend continued remote surveillance. P.S. Please tell Bruce we expect a bonus for hazardous quantum exposure.

If that was such a thing.

She reached the galley, crossing past the little nook with its battered orange bench cushions and dull gray table, the same one she'd eaten at, argued with Spike at, and, once, hidden under during a daytime nightmare. A spider bot hung off the galley counter, five of its eight spindly legs splayed, polishing a mug. As soon as she stepped too close, it chirped, whirred, set the mug down, and zoomed off. Some things never changed.

Frankie rifled through the small Kroll box of supplies Scarlett had sent with her from White Moon. The cream-and-orange crate was labeled "Fragile—Lab Materials."

Frankie rolled her eyes. She'd asked for a jar of that green soup, and the recipe.

She popped the latches, and a waft of cold, slightly medicinal air floated out. On top was a bag of hydroponic mineral powder, two protein bars taped together with a sticky note ("You said you liked the peanut" in Scarlett's scrawl, "Nobody here does."). Under that, the jar of soup, and a small clear dome. Inside the dome, a seedling, its roots spiraling through gel, a pale green shoot curling up, tipped with red.

Tucked in beside it was a second note, this one from Tala:

For the Spear—adapts to shipboard light, and doesn't mind zero-g. Keep somewhere you can see it change. P.S. If you need a new lab assistant, you know where to find me.

Frankie grinned and ran a thumb over the condensation on the dome. "Welcome aboard," she whispered. Her heart did a weird little flip, like gravity had shifted.

She dug deeper—plastic crinkling, the smell of industrial printer ink sharp in her nose. At the bottom of the box, under a false insert, something else: a half-used can of "Blue Sky" wall paint, and another of "Butter morning." Taped to the blue can:

"Go on. Make it yours. —Marsh"

Frankie closed her eyes and pictured the way those yellow-cream conference walls glowed under the lab lights, how homely the galley could feel with a lick of something warmer than functional gray.

She carried a steaming mug of coffee and her new plant-friend over to her nook, and tucked herself in.

A familiar yowl sounded from the corridor. Spike padded in, tail up, fur in wild tufts—half brushed, half rebellious, the stripes on her back shining from the ship's recycled sunlight. She stopped dead in the galley's threshold, eyeing Frankie like she'd been caught plotting a mutiny.

"Need another spa day?" Frankie teased.

Spike shook out more of her fur—blasted it out, really. Disreputable beast.

Frankie nestled deeper into the cozy eating nook, sinking gratefully into the ugly cushions. Someday, maybe new ones, navy. Or henna red. The coffee, laced with peppermint from her prized stash, warmed her fingers. Curls of steam rose gently, minty good.

Spike perched comfortably behind Frankie's head, a velvety guardian atop the bench back. Frankie reached back, hoping to offer scritches, but Spike batted her hand away.

After all, she had just suggested another spa day.

Scarlett herself had walked them to the moon's big elevator. She'd brushed invisible dust from Frankie's sleeve, given Spike a dignified nod, and said not to worry about Tala. "Officially, she's on probation. But Kara's not letting go of talent like that," she'd said, unable to fully hide her happiness.

"So she's staying." Frankie said, smiling at Scarlett's absolute glow.

"You know what she told me? 'When we change the universe, I want to do it standing next to you—not over you, not instead of you. Together." She sighed.

Frankie was a little shocked at how quickly the team had re-formed after everything. Then again, it made sense. Prakara Gold and Tala Foss, bright and wild and determined, would be changing the universe. Better they do it together.

Jan Wint, meanwhile, had made her intentions quietly clear. She'd be taking the first official Cooperative District to the capital, determined, now, to be an advocate from the inside—"someone has to tell the truth," Wint had said, managing a rare, tight smile. "And, let's be honest, if Gold's happy hidden out here, I might finally get the position I've deserved for years."

The Skolls—who now knew everyone on base knew they knew about the transmitter—were due tomorrow. Huxley Parker, failed double-agent, would face whatever edge-space justice that meant. Frankie didn't envy him that future.

She felt the floor vibrate gently. Ship breaking orbit. Shifting course to angle for the jump gate. She called up a view screen showing the rear-facing camera.

White Moon Landing spun away, already receding into the glittering darkness.

Squinting, Frankie pretended she could see the faint outline of the station's donuts, especially the one farthest out.

Then they were gone.

Her wristcom beeped, and beeped again. And again.

Guess they were out of the no-comms range.

She called up her messages. Bruce's note blinked at her, obnoxiously red, but she ignored it in favor of her friend Beth's: *Call me. No, it's good news.*

The ship chimed softly, Ship's voice filtered through the overhead: "Course locked. Three hours forty-eight minutes to the first jump gate. Smooth as vacuum, Captain."

Frankie grinned. "Music, please. Something with a little bounce."

The room filled with the soft, percussive pulse of old station pop. Frankie leaned her head gently back on Spike's warm flank and just…breathed. The galley's walls gleamed in the ship's light, waiting for a splash of color. She could almost see the future: blue here, yellow there, a sunburst over the entry arch.

She needed more colors.

She could already picture Tala's plant vining its way up the wall, curling around whatever color she chose.

Go on. Make it yours.

A beep from her wristcom: another incoming. Bruce, again. Frankie sighed, but didn't get up. "Not yet," she said aloud. "First things first."

She poured fresh water for Spike, who sniffed at it and promptly stuck a paw in the bowl, flicking droplets in all directions. Frankie laughed, the sound bouncing off the bare walls, the kind of laugh you only give yourself when you know you're safe —as safe as you can be in the wild weirdness of space.

"Trouble," Spike growled, shaking her paw, eyes glinting. Frankie raised her mug in salute, the warmth spooling out through her fingers.

"Your turn to call Bruce."

The Spear sailed on, her walls waiting for paint, her hydroponics growing, Spike's fur already everywhere.

And three gates' worth of star-bright possibility ahead.

ALSO BY NICKY PENTTILA

Cosmic Weave

Cooperative Realm: Frankie's Journeys
Cargo Trouble

Frankie Takes a Holiday

Frankie Takes a Dive

Frankie Finds a Dot

Frankie Takes a Bow

Cargo & Chaos: Frankie books 1 & 2

Cooperative Realm: The Arkhide Chronicles
Hidden Planet

The Listeners

The Elders of Arkhide

Tales of Arkhide story collection

Historical Fiction
A Note of Scandal

An Untitled Lady

The Spanish Patriot

ABOUT THE AUTHOR

Nicky Penttila wrote her first story, a Mayan murder mystery, in seventh grade. But then came gymnastics, math team, and boyfriends. Later came husband, car payments, and a sleep-depriving work schedule at newspapers across the country. Then came a second career as a science writer. But the fiction kept trickling out, a story here, a novella there, and finally, a real live novel. And she hasn't stopped.

Find more great reads at nickypenttila.com